Milk, Turkey, and Neurosis

Or, How Mother (Almost) Ruined My Life

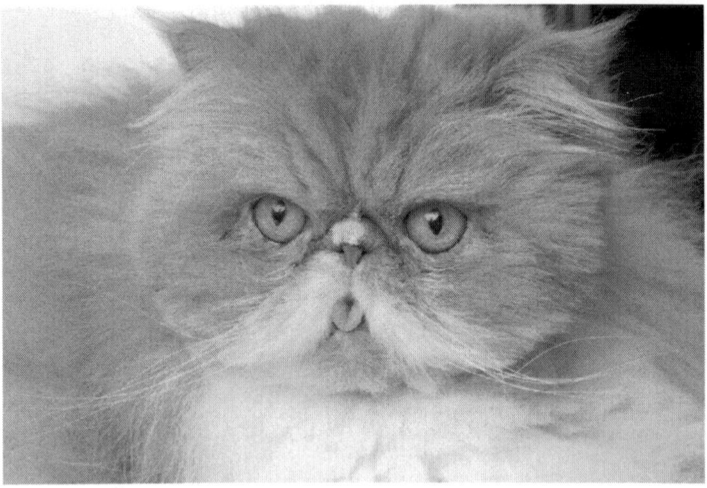

Milk, Turkey, and Neurosis

Or, How Mother (Almost) Ruined My Life

By Grace Feldman

Phase II Publishing ☺ Ft. Lauderdale, FL

THIS IS AN ABOUT PHASE BOOK PUBLISHED BY PHASE II PUBLISHING

This is a work of fiction. Names, characters, places, and incidents are either the product of the author's imagination or are used fictitiously. Any resemblance to actual persons, living or dead, events, or locales, is entirely coincidental.

Text copyright © 2014 by Giovanni V. Crisan

Jacket Artwork © 2014 by Giovanni V. Crisan

Cover Art © 2014 by Giovanni V. Crisan

Grace Feldman Photo © 2014 by Minemero / istockphoto

Morgott Photo © 2009 by jclegg / istockphoto

All rights reserved.

No part of this book may be used or reproduced in any manner whatsoever without written permission except in the case of brief quotations embodied in critical articles and reviews.

Published in the United States by Phase II Publishing, Ft. Lauderdale.

ABOUT PHASE is a trademark of Phase II Publishing.

Designed and edited by Giovanni V. Crisan

SUMMARY:

Gracie Feldman is cursed. Her mother's blundering impudence seems to sabotage every job, every relationship, and every aspect of her life. Now Gracie is living single, with her obese, feebleminded, lazy cat Morgott in an apartment in Fort Lauderdale, Florida, and Thanksgiving is quickly approaching. Gracie knows Mother will soon call with an invitation to the holiday dinner, and she will not let the twenty-something girl live it down if she shows up without a date; so she rashly tells Dearest Mother that she already has a boyfriend. Gracie has to scramble and embark on a series of blind dates to find someone who could not only survive Mother's bumbles, but would receive Mother's approval.

As the clock winds closer to the eleventh hour, Gracie's blind date debacles, ranging from a cross-dressing police officer to a mustached marauder to a heavyset swinger who lives with an elderly couple, have landed her on desperate grounds. Now Gracie's dignity and future hangs on this dinner going perfectly, to try and find sanity before insanity finds her.

Colorful characters that range from a cat who is entranced by its own shadow, an aunt who speaks her own language, and a girl who needs to find her own life fill the story like the stuffing in a Thanksgiving turkey.

Join Gracie and her kooky cat Morgott in their search for a man, a career, a life, and a delicious dinner Gracie can call her own.

ISBN: **978-1495986888**

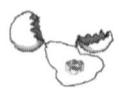

Printed in the United States of America

First Phase II Publishing trade paperback edition February 2014

For my mother, Mallory, without whom this book would not be possible.

Chapter 1

Sunday, October 26

Five Lessons From Mother

As I sit and write this profile I am looking at my cat, Morgott, jump from the windowsill to my bed, then to my nightstand, and then flat on his face against the floor. Never mind the fact that he's fat and clumsy, he's also dumb. So dumb that I often find him staring at his own shadow for several minutes at a time. He's eight years old, he should have learned by now that he has a freakin' shadow. But this has been my life. I have learned many things that will help me one day, but the most important ones came from my mother.

My mother used to say, "Gracie," she would say, "you must learn these little lessons that nobody is going to teach you in life [I wish I knew why when I was a kid]. And one day, these will help you out of a tight spot." So here, in all their glory, are my mother's top life lessons. Read with caution.

1. **When you can't brush your teeth, chew on grass**. I don't know where she got this

crazy idea, but my mother's first lesson did me no favors in elementary and middle school. As a kid you tend to forget quite often to brush your teeth in the morning. So I would confidently arrive at school and head straight for the grass. I would drop to my knees and grab handfuls of it and shovel it into my mouth, chewing it for a few minutes, then spitting it out. It never occurred to me that nobody else was doing this, and I would spend the entire day with green teeth. It wasn't until Mrs. Delaney saw me one morning in seventh grade that I learned the awful truth. My reputation followed me through high school, and I was unaware of my nickname until a "typo" appeared under my picture my senior year, naming me "Grazer Feldman."

2. **If you run out of gas, get a man to pee in your tank.** *Thanks mom, for that timeless piece of wisdom. My car exploded, ok? MY CAR EXPLODED. The guy who peed in my tank? Yeah, he had tried to warn me, but I assured him I knew what I was doing; I told him I had years of experience fixing cars. I forced him to do it, even as he warned me that my engine would stop working if he showered it with gold. I cheered him on, Mother. And worse, as my car burned to a crisp on the side of the highway, the guy - who was very cute, by the*

way - chuckled and told me it <u>sucks to be me.</u> Then he asked me where I learned about cars. I had to make up a ridiculous lie - I told him it was in Kantucker, Kentucky (where I was from - ?), and I was forced to tell him our cars ran on pee 'up them parts'. Then I had to awkwardly ride in his car the whole way to the next town, 55 miles away.

3. Get a cat. Get several cats. They are smarter than you, and if you want to get smart, you need to start spending time with others who are smarter than you. *Well, I already told you about Morgott, so we really don't need to go there, but my mother had two cats, "East" and "West"; so named because each one sat on one of her shoulders. What I always thought, though, was that whenever my mother was facing east or west, the cats should be named "North" and "South". After raising Morgott I realized how my mother got so smart.*

4. When you dance, always keep one hand on your waist - it keeps you looking feminine. *Oh, college. Imagine seeing a girl who looks like the Chiquita Banana lady on the dance floor every night. I know, a woman with bananas on her head is not what college guys are looking for when they go out to a club.*

Sure, I didn't really have bananas on my head, but dancing with my hand on my waist the entire time, did I really need bananas?

5. When you go to the beach, wear knee-high boots, it keeps the sharks from recognizing that you're alive. Yeah, sharks and nearly every other living thing on the planet! Not to mention how difficult it was to walk out of the ocean with boots full of water. I just Googled "weirdoes at the beach" for shats and gaggles and found TWELVE videos of myself, labeled "Return of the Living March of the Penguins".

Yes, that's ME waddling like Frankenstein's monster out of the water. They have made an entire video series of me at the beach. Different boots, same idiot. Screw you sharks. It's all your fault.

Now that I think about it, how am I still sane? Anyway, if you ever catch yourself chewing on grass while you pee in your gas tank with a hand on your waist, a cat on your shoulder, and wearing knee-high boots, hit me up. We could totally hang.

Yes, Mother

I closed my almost-obsolete computer and walked to the kitchen to grab some milk. Morgott was in the corner, staring at his shadow as usual, cocking his head to one side, then the other, trying to figure out what it was he was looking at. I hoped that he was simply entranced by the blinking umbrage - an illusion resulting from the pairing of the blades of the ceiling fan in my living room and its attached light. But I knew better. I let out an exasperated breath, then opened my fridge and saw that I was almost out of milk, so I made a mental note to get more later.

As I sipped my milk, I shot a nervous glance at my cellphone. Like a hot coal it pulsated, illuminating as a reminder (as if I needed a reminder), that I had a voice message waiting. And like with a hot coal, I didn't want to touch it. The message was from my mother.

I wasn't ready at the moment to go through the grand inquisition that I suffered every time I spoke with her.

I wanted to at least land a date before Thanksgiving because I knew my mother would be asking who I was seeing and demand to meet him. I couldn't go another year as a single 28 year-old for all the major holidays, so I was desperate.

My focus zoomed to the Dell laptop, my Millionaire Matchmaker, resting on my mahogany desk across from the kitchen and entrance of my modest apartment. Hopefully my sob story would get me a couple of pity dates from the DatesUnlimited website, on which I was now a proud Platinum Member, and who knows? Maybe I'd find someone special. But for now I needed to get my mind off the website. And my mother.

Twirling round, I scanned the room and honed-in on the two black garbage bags full of useless items I had by the door and thought I'd kill some time by taking them to the Salvation Nation for donation (yay, that rhymed!).

Getting rid of my old clothes and household items was refreshing and cathartic. Plus, if I was going to have a guy over, I couldn't let him see my old clothes; and I definitely couldn't let him see the coffee-stained, crocheted mantel my grandmother had given me as a debutante gift when I landed my first real job. I was supposed to drape it over the tablecloth on my kitchen table; I was too lazy to hand-wash it and too scared to stick the thing in the machine whe I spilled the coffee on it. Besides, it was hideous, and I'd only used it once. It was obviously God who moved my hand to spill my *cafè con leche* on it, and I decided that rather than wash it, I'd heed His omen and donate it.

Hoping that the hour I'd be gone would give a few guys time to find my profile, I lugged the bags into my car, one at a time, down three floors in the sauna they called an elevator. Within the hour those old musty rags, batter-coated whisks, my old rusty toaster, and the smoothie maker that I never used, were gone. A year ago I wouldn't have dreamed of discarding these relics from my college days.

My mother would have killed me if she'd known I'd donated stuff without washing it first. She had her way of doing things, and really had no connection to the modern world. I was sure the Salvation Nation had some streamlined way of cleaning everything they received before putting it out on the sales floor. It only made sense that they would, otherwise they'd be asking for a lawsuit every time they sold some garment infested with bed bugs or some blender laced with salmonella.

When I got back home, I immediately checked to see if I'd had any replies to my online ad, but alas, I hadn't received any. *Stupid, Gracie*, I thought, *you need to put a picture on your profile! People probably think you're a Hungry Hungry Hippo that doesn't even fit in a standard-sized picture.*

I quickly sorted through all the pictures I had of myself on my computer, and found that the best one was of me with my mother and my best friend Herbie at my college graduation. The sky in the background was blue with pinkish-orange, common at dusk. I was wearing my glasses, which I usually don't like to wear, but I thought I looked particularly cute - kind of like Mayim Bialik. I had my hair straight, and I was wearing a cute yellow summer dress, cut a few inches above the knee.

My mother, on the other hand, had her hair up like Marge Simpson from the cartoons, except her hair wasn't cerulean like the character: it was a Dracula red - almost orange. She wore her glasses, too, even though she only needed them to read. She always said they made her look more scholarly. She also had a neon pink cord attached to each leg of the glasses and around her neck. Her grass-colored blouse was yet another token of embarrassment, not only because it made her hair color significantly more pronounced, but because it had gaudy ruffles along the neckline that, along with her meaty figure, made her look like a mutant Faverolles chicken.

After cringing, I cropped her out of the picture, although her bright red press-on nails were ever-present in the image, on my shoulder where she had her arm around me.

Blue-eyed Herbie stood to my left in the picture. He was my best friend growing up, and we were each other's support system through the hard times. His eyes were like sapphires, and almost demanded all the attention in the picture. Almost. He was so fat that half of him was already out of the picture, so I just cropped the rest of him out. I couldn't have guys think I was the victim of two ravenous buffalo. I looked so, "eyelash on a cow" next to them - completely invisible. Herbie had to be sacrificed for the sake of my future and my sanity. He was such a nice guy, though. Gay guys usually are.

I uploaded my new-born masterpiece of a picture and tapped my fist against the table. *This should do it*, I thought. *There will be one less single girl in Fort Lauderdale this Thanksgiving*!

Monday, October 27

The First

The next day I woke up early, before the sun came up. Call it superstition, but I didn't look at my emails right away; instead, I decided to go for a morning walk. I always thought that if you jump the gun on something you really want, then it will be disappointing, so I always knew that if I delayed gratification, it would be to my own benefit.

Morgott was on the couch as usual, and I had to grab the lint brush to lift most of his dark orange and white hair off of it. I passed the sticky roller over the seat of the couch, and when I tried to get the area under him, Morgott yawned and refused to move.

"You bum," I said with a smile. I tossed the lint brush back into the corner of the living room and headed out the door.

During my walk I realized everything seemed much brighter and more colorful than usual. It was definitely a sign that my plan was working, and that this would be a great new beginning in my life. The birds were chirping, and the street corners were full of kids waiting to be picked up by the buses to take them to school. A refreshing breeze glazed over my face and body, carrying with it the briny smell of the ocean.

A palm tree, which was just slightly taller than my mother when I was a kid, now loomed at almost twice my height. Memories fulminated in my brain, and I felt nostalgic. I used to stand on that very corner in Pompano with my best friend Herbie all the way through high school.

He was a nice kid, and I think we became friends because other kids picked on both of us at school. He was fat, and I had the embarrassment that was my mother. We met in second grade, and later found out we lived near each other.

"Lazy Gracie, Lazy Gracie," my classmates chanted one time when I fell asleep during fourth grade.

"Leave her alone!" said Herbie when the kids did it again in the cafeteria. When they didn't stop, he dumped his chocolate milk on the floor behind them.

"Don't worry, Gracie, I wouldn't have drank it anyway," he told me when I offered him mine. The bullies got in trouble, because the monitor thought they'd had a food fight.

The following day the bullies retaliated by giving Herbie a wedgie; it was so bad his underpants ripped and the bullies spread a rumor that they'd ripped because he was so fat. "Don't worry Herb," I assured him, "I'll get them back for you this time."

So the next day I walked in with laxative chocolate bars to "make peace" with the bullies. It didn't stop them from bothering us, but revenge sure was *sweet*.

We became like siblings, he my shoulder to cry on when my mother did something embarrassing, and I was there for him when kids at school teased him or when his volatile parents had a spat. I missed him; we hadn't seen each other since my college graduation.

Outside my apartment building, I thought to please the powers-that-be and increase my fortunes by delaying my return a bit more. So I climbed up and down the stairs five times. A total of fifteen flights is pretty darn good; my personal trainer would be proud - if I had a personal trainer.

This was great for when it rained out, which happened often in South Florida. It was easy to exercise in my apartment building in this way, because all the old Jewish retirees seemed attracted to this particular building, and they never used the stairs. Although I knew South Florida was known for drawing elders like turkeys to Thanksgiving tables, people always stuck with their own kind, and the Jewish elders were no exception.

Inside my apartment, I could see my computer directly across from the front door beckoning me once again, sitting like the Venus fly trap in *The Little Shop of Horrors*. *"Feed me, Seymour!"* But I resisted. I really, really wanted to show the powers that be that I could make the necessary sacrifices to get what I wanted; so I ignored it and hopped in the shower.

While the steam caressed my face and the warm water embraced my body, I thought about my future; if I found a boyfriend, all would be good. I had a decent job, even though everyone thought I was a weirdo because of Linda and what happened during my interview. But in the end, the job allowed me to live on my own and be a responsible adult. Best yet, it allowed me to put a chasm, albeit small, between me and my mother.

I got out of the shower and saw Morgott sitting on his butt with his head against the wall like a junkie in some Manhattan alley. Such an oddball.

I put on my "good luck" underwear: a lacy yellow and black bikini panty and a matching bra. Then I sorted through a few outfits: *too dark, too tight, too revealing*. They went straight to my floor as I knocked them off the list of possibility for the day. Finally I narrowed my choices to four tops and three bottoms. I tried on all of them, and decided on a royal blue blouse and gray trousers.

I headed to the kitchen, ignoring my red "Dell From Hell", ate a delicious breakfast of Cookie Crisp with the last of the milk, and finally I was ready to roll on another day at Graduate Plastics.

Before I ran out the door, I finally gave in and rushed over to my computer to check if I had received any emails from DatesUnlimited. Sure enough, I had three replies. One of the guys was fat and ugly, one looked like he was eight, and the third guy was dreamy. He was perfect: beautiful olive skin, a trendy short spiky hairstyle, nice designer clothes, a buff body, and standing on the aft of a yacht. *Hopefully that's his boat*, I thought.

I clicked on the link to read what he had to say. *Take Me Out... Of My Misery!* it started. Ok, not hilarious, but it sounded like he had a sense of humor. I continued reading. *My name is Elmer and I live on my yacht,* My Misery. *I'm looking for a girl who doesn't take herself too seriously and wants to have fun while we (hopefully) forge something more serious. So come on, take me out of* My Misery, *and I just may take you on it.*

Ok, the rest of the message was better, but I was still a little iffy about him. I clicked on "reply" and started typing. *Hi Elmer, I'm Gracie and I got your message. I must say, it sounds a little generic though. Are you a real person or are you a robot? And, please define "fun" so I can decide if you're a weirdo or not.*

I sent the message and went off to work. My day dragged slower than peanut butter out of an upside-down jar. Despite this, I continued my Shaolin-like ritual and robbed myself of instant gratification again by going to the grocery store after I got off work.

While the smell of the tropics engulfed me and the automatic misters they used on the vegetables tickled my face in the produce section, I grabbed a head of lettuce and tore off a leaf, then placed the leaf over a tomato. All I could think about while shopping was being in a cute new designer bikini holding a champagne flute, leaning against the railing on Elmer's wonderful yacht. The waves of the ocean behind us, creating a wonderful symphony for our wonderful life together.

"Excuse me," said an old woman trying to grab some lettuce herself. I looked around and saw that people stared at me like I was insane, holding tomatoes covered in lettuce against my chest, but I didn't care. This was going to be my year of resolution, and I'd soon have a future they'd all be jealous of.

When I returned home, I realized I'd forgotten to buy milk again but I shrugged off the thought; I rushed to my computer to see if he'd responded. The page loaded and I saw that he had replied. Yay! Like a frantic woman fighting for a bouquet at a wedding, I quickly opened the message, clicked on the link, and devoured his reply.

*Hi **Gracie**. Thanks for your reply, **Gracie**. As you can see I'm not a robot. I would love to be the glue that holds your life together, **Gracie**. We can form a "bond" that would never be broken (but is washable!). Hit me up, **Gracie**.*

*Oh, and fun is: a feeling provided by anything that is entertaining or amusing; providing enjoyment. Hope that helps with your homework, **Gracie**.*

-Elmer

Alright, he was being obnoxious, yet humorous. I guess I did ask for it when I called him a generic robot. In any case, I replied again.

***Elmer**: Thanks for the definition. I don't know why I couldn't find it. Do you just want a pen pal or are you looking to actually meet? You didn't ask for my number or anything. And is that really <u>your</u> yacht in the picture? Don't lie now and get yourself into a "sticky" situation. -Gracie*

I put the groceries away, which took several minutes, then I peeked in my bedroom to see if

I could gather the motivation to wash some clothes, but there were piles of clean and dirty clothes all over the floor around my bed. Ugh. I closed the door and went back to my living area, and when I returned to my Dell, I saw he had responded.

Gracie, I will meet you at Restaurant de Rêves *on Thursday at 7. And yes, that's* my *yacht. I think that you're the one that's not a real person; you're more like a year-old egg, because you're full of bad jokes. -Elmer*

Cute, I thought. Then it hit me. *Oh, man, a date! What would I wear? Oh my God, I haven't done my hair, either. I'll have to spend all day tomorrow getting fixed up and shopping for a dress.*

"Morgott," I said to my loyal cat, "I have a date!"

He looked at me and then looked away, disinterested.

"Oh, don't be jealous. It's gonna be exciting!"

Restaurant de Rêves. The place sounded fancy, and since he owned a yacht, I knew I had to go all-out. In total I spent about $600 getting prepared for this date, between getting my hair done and buying that sexy *Gianet Garçon* dress and matching purse. *He better look like his picture,* I thought, *and he better pay for the dinner.*

My fear of dating would finally be laid to rest, along with the painful memories of past disasters. My mother always blamed *me* when a date went to the food processor, but all of my dating woes could be attributed to how she ruined my first.

Freshman Year, High School

The Panties

I could smell the cleaning solvent, lemon-scented of course, in the driveway outside our house. I looked over at Ron and smiled. I knew that my mother was cleaning, which would mean two things: 1.) the place would look great when Ron walked in, and 2.) Mother would be out of our way while we watched a movie.

I looked up and gawked at our Salvador Dali-like Florida skyline. I reached for my key and placed it in the keyhole, and just before I turned it, I closed my eyes and prayed that she didn't do anything that would humiliate me.

Before I opened the door I looked over at Ron one more time and pecked him on the lips as a way to reassure myself that everything would be ok no matter what. He was a Junior, which meant I was lucky to be on a date with him, and I really needed to make a good impression. So with fingers crossed I opened the door and we entered.

As soon as we walked in I saw my mother, who had her back to us, cleaning the wood dinner table by the entrance. She was in a light blue nightgown and pink slippers, which was her uniform when cleaning.

"Hi, mother," I said. "This is Ron, the guy I've been telling you about." She stopped what she was doing and turned around at the snap of a camera.

"Hi, Mrs. Feldman," Ron said, extending his hand.

"Hi Dear! I've heard so much about you," said my mother while vigorously shaking Ron's hand.

"Ditto," replied Ron.

"Mother, we're gonna watch a movie," I said as I walked away.

We went straight to the couch, where Ron immediately made his place. I didn't sit; rather, I went into the kitchen and called out, "What would you like to drink?"

"I'll have a soda, thanks," he said.

I pulled a canned soda from the fridge and got a diet one for myself, then headed back to the couch. Ron had already turned on the TV, and was watching football. I sat down and still managed to ask, "So whatcha watching?"

"The Pacers game," he replied.

"Who's winning?"

"We are. Thirty-two to fourteen," he replied.

"Hey, do you maybe wanna watch a movie?"

"Sure, whatever you want," he said. I pecked him on the cheek to let him know that I appreciated his giving up watching his game to appease me.

"Why don't you offer him something to drink," called out my mother, who was still cleaning in the dining area.

"I already did, mother," I called back.

I placed my hand on Ron's lap and looked at him with a smile on my face. His cold brown eyes betrayed his gentle character. I looked at the skin on his face and noticed every nick and cut; my father had once told me that men didn't need beauty products because they naturally exfoliated their skin when they shaved. I don't know how true that was, because many boys have bad acne, but not Ron; although he was yet to master the art of shaving. He was so intent on finding a movie to watch and didn't seem to notice me staring at him.

"Aha! 'Suspect Zero'," he said triumphantly.

"Aw, can we maybe watch something a little less serious?" I asked.

He looked over at me and started to say something in protest, but instead smiled and nodded.

"How 'bout 'Skeletal Remains'?" he said. I gave him a look, then noticed the wry smile on his face.

"Just kidding. Let's watch 'Dirty Dancing' then," he said.

"Why don't you offer him something to eat," called out my mother, again from the obscured dining room.

I slumped my shoulders, looked left toward the dining area, and let out a breath. "Would you like something to eat," I asked my date.

"Yeah, sure. Just like chips or something," he replied.

I got up and Ron immediately flipped the TV back to the football game. *It's ok*, I thought, *it's still going great, fingers crossed*. I grabbed a bag of chips and a jar of salsa and brought them back to the couch.

"Come on catch it, catch it!" Ron called out as if he was coaching the game himself.

I stared at him, admiring how his dark, wavy hair bounced when he screamed and jerked around in protest of his team's bad decisions.

"Are we going to watch that movie?" I asked.

"Huh? Oh yeah, sorry," he said, grabbing a chip, dipping it in salsa, and putting it in his mouth before changing the channel. I found it cute when some salsa dripped on his t-shirt and avalanched down to his jeans. Then I grabbed a chip and was about to dip it in the salsa when again called mother.

"Did you put the chips and salsa in a bowl?" She called out to me. Why couldn't she just let me live my *life*?

I got up yet again, taking the chips and salsa with me so I could serve them the way my mother wanted. On my way to the kitchen, I could hear Ron change the TV back to the football game.

I pulled two bowls out of the cupboard and poured the chips into one and the salsa into the other. I opened the fridge to see if we had any other dipping sauces I could offer Ron. I saw a block of cheddar cheese and thought it would be a great idea to melt that into the salsa and make *queso* dip, so I placed the entire block in the bowl and stuck it into the microwave.

After two minutes, I could smell the cheese and the salsa; finally there was something delicious to cover up the strong odor of lemon-fresh bleach. The microwave beeped and I pulled out my concoction. The cheese was still whole. I put the bowl back in and set the timer to two minutes again.

I was waiting for forever.

Finally the microwave beeped and, as I opened the microwave door, I could hear my mother calling out, "He'll like it if you melt some cheese and mix it in some salsa for dipping the chips. The Mexicans call it *contesso* dip." Her high-pitch tone always made her sound like she was asking a question.

"Yes, Mother," I called out, with a little annoyance evident in my tone. "I'm already doing that. And it's called *queso* dip."

"What? No sweetie," she said. "That's where Barefoot Contessa gets her name. She makes *contesso* dip."

Ugh. Whatever, it was pointless; I turned to look at the bowl, and was startled by Ron's hulking figure. I placed a hand on my chest and said, "Oh my God, you scared me."

"I'm not *that* ugly am I?"

I laughed. "I'm making some *queso* dip. How's the game going?"

"It's on commercials right now, Mrs. *Contessa*, ha ha," he said as he leaned in to kiss me.

His lips were soft and warm; his tongue was like a feather as it danced with mine, like peacocks in a mating dance. Then I remembered my mother was there and could walk in on us at any moment. Instantly I pulled away and held both hands up, saying, "Go go go, I'll be right out."

He returned to the living room and I looked down at the dip and saw that the cheese still hadn't melted. *What the heck*? It was like trying to melt a cinder block! I stuck it back in the microwave and set it to three minutes this time to make sure that sucker was done.

While the microwave plate turned and made its whirring sound I turned around and leaned back against the counter, thinking of Ron. What kind of husband would he make? He was a regular guy with the football obsession and all, yet he was kind and thoughtful. "Gracie and Ron" - it had a nice ring to it.

The microwave beeped again and I turned around to see my masterwork of culinary genius. Upon opening the microwave door, however, I saw that the darn cheese was still mostly a big, cold block. *Ugh*, I thought in frustration, *you're gonna melt for me just like Ron is gonna melt for me!* So I stuck it in and hit five minutes on the timer. Ha. If that didn't do it, I didn't know what would.

"Aw, man! That wasn't a penalty!" I could hear Ron screaming again at the TV.

"Make sure you dice up the cheese so it can melt, and only put a little at a time," called my mother in her New York accent. Her shrill voice even made the air cringe.

"Mother! I know what I'm doing! I'm not an idiot!" I screamed. I was fed up.

Just then, Ron grabbed me from behind, put his hands around my waist, and began to kiss my neck. I tightened up 'cause it was tickling me, but it felt so good; oh, it felt good. Closing my eyes, I gave in to the simple pleasures of youthful innocence.

His breath sounded like the waves of the ocean; it felt like the warm, soft fingers of a baby. And his body felt hard but comforting, like a firm mattress. Then I felt his hand gliding seamlessly under my t-shirt, soft and self-assured, past my bellybutton as I reflexively sucked my stomach in, the fingers never stopping for a break, over my ribs, where they turned back toward my belly button to tease before continuing their odyssey upwards. I felt his excitement behind me just as a chill ran at the base of my neck, and I took a deep, slow, satisfying breath.

Then, without warning, there was a loud *bang!* and a *plop!* from inside the microwave. Shaking Ron's hands off me, I quickly turned and opened the microwave door only to find burnt salsa and bubbling cheese all over the inside, and the bowl, which was cracked in half.

"Whoa," said Ron when he saw the mess.

Just then, my mother frenzied into the kitchen, asking, "What was that noise?"

When she saw what I'd done, she began her usual rant. "You didn't follow my instructions and now look at what I have to clean when I just cleaned that microwave and that kitchen and cheese is so hard to scrape off of things you never listen Gracie!"

She pushed past me and Ron, still ranting, and didn't allow me a second to say that I would clean it up. She waved the rag she had in her hand and started to scrub the inside of the microwave with it. "We need to clean this before it dries."

Ron, being the sweet boy I knew him to be, placed a hand on my mother's back and reached in the microwave for the rag. "Don't stress, Mrs. Feldman, I got this."

When he pulled the rag out to rinse it under the faucet, I realized it was one of my panties! *Oh God, why?* Ron immediately realized what they were and held them up, all full of cheese and with a streak mark in the back. There was no denying they were mine, because I was so skinny and my mother was heavyset. There was no way out of it. I wanted to stick my head inside the microwave and set it to eternal frying.

"Oh my God, Mother! Why on earth are you using my underwear to clean?" I screamed in horror. Tears were now welled up in my eyes because I knew I was defeated and this would be the last I'd hear from Ron.

"Why not," she said in her New York Jewish accent, "those were stained in the back and I couldn't get the stain out so I use it as a rag." The hard "G" that New York Jews are known for always made me think of a tiger growling my name, because when a sentence ended in that hard "G", it was always trouble. For me.

"I tried bleach, vinegar, nothing worked. I don't know what you ate that day."

"Mother!" I screamed in humiliation, and covered my face with my hands. If it wasn't over after he saw my cheesy, streak-marked underwear, it was definitely over now that he heard I stained my underwear so bad that my mother couldn't get it off with all sorts of chemicals. I snatched the panties from Ron's hands and rushed to my room, slammed the door, and locked it.

I picked up the phone and dialed Herbie to tell him of my mother's latest antics.

"Herbie," I managed between sobs, "she's done it, she's ruined my life!"

"Grace," he replied. "Calm down and tell me what happened."

"She humiliated me in front of Ron and now I'll be alone forever."

"Look, don't worry about it. Whatever it was, it can't be so bad that he won't ever talk to you again. And if he doesn't, then you know something important about him; something that you can think about when you ask yourself if you really wanted to date a guy like that. Your mother will always be there, and whoever is meant for you will have to accept her. Craziness and all."

He always knew what to say. "Thanks Herbie."

As I hung up the phone, I let out a breath. I felt good, relaxed. At least for that moment, everything seemed alright. Then I heard her voice.

My mother was talking to Ron, saying, "I'm not sure what's gotten into her. She's never acted like this about me using her stained underwears for cleaning before. I don't know what's happening." Hard. "G".

Chapter 2

Thursday, October 30

The Mustache

The day had finally come and I was running like a bee around a disturbed hive. This was the night I was going to meet Mr. Elmer, the future glue of my life.

I called my friend Jennifer to tell her the good news the day before, and she'd given me some sound advice.

"Be upfront with him," she told me. "Tell him your mother is crazy and that way he'll be prepared when he meets her. Give him some ;examples, tell him about things she's done to drive away other men in your life. And don't invite him to Thanksgiving after one date! You need to go on at least three before you drop something like that on a guy."

Determined to make this the last time I'd have to make a first impression on a guy, I put on my new designer dress and looked in the mirror. The dress looked really good on me, and my butt didn't look as flat as it usually did, the girls didn't look so small, and the dress hugged my slight curves in just the right areas. It was worth every cent I paid for it.

I still had twenty minutes before I had to leave, but I felt rushed. I hurried to my bedroom; my modest twin-sized bed was in turmoil, with clothes all over the floor. Some were dirty, others were clothes I'd tried on before work that didn't make the cut on that particular day. I convinced myself that this was my unconscious mind creating a way for me to avoid making a mistake on a first date.

I stepped over the mess and went to my vanity to find some earrings and a necklace that would complement my new dress and purse without overpowering them. All of my fine jewelry was originally my mother's - she always gave me one of her pieces of jewelry on the last day of Hanukkah. It was a nice thought, as she was trying to make heirlooms out of her frippery, but most of it was simply not my style.

I decided I'd have to wear something fake. I tried on six different necklaces and three different sets of earrings before narrowing it down to two of each. *Red or blue*? I thought. Ruby would probably make too much of a statement and overpower my black dress, so I decided on sapphire.

I checked my hair and makeup three more times in the bathroom mirror to make sure everything was perfect.

"Morgott," I said, "wish me luck!"

He looked at me from the couch, then fixed his gaze on me until I walked out the door. If he was any other animal, I would probably be concerned that he was planning to do something bad while I was gone, but this was Morgott we were talking about here.

I headed out to the restaurant, guided by my trusty phone GPS.

The traffic wasn't bad; rush hour had just subsided, and most cars were heading *away* from downtown, I was aiming *for* it. The sun was just starting to set, so the view was still of homeless people and drug addicts in the more nondescript streets. At night, downtown came alive with lights, restaurants, and of course, Las Olas, the tourism magnet of Fort Lauderdale.

So there I was, ready to walk into the *Restaurant de Rêves* and meet the man of my dreams. I looked one more time at his profile picture on my phone, closed my eyes, and took a deep breath.

Nice, I thought. *Smells like Europe.*

A big smile was on my face when I reached for the door. "Allow me," exclaimed the doorman who then reached for and opened it for me. I hadn't even noticed him standing there.

"Oh, thank you," I said.

"Pas de quoi," he replied, tipping his hat, and I blushed.

Elmer, I thought, *I really hope I'm your type*.

I entered and found the place to be less formal than I thought it would be. There were people in t-shirts, and here I was in a fancy black dress. Ugh. The bar was right by the entrance, so I walked over and sat on a stool. I ordered a diet soda from Gary, the burly bartender, and looked around as I sipped it through the straw he'd given me.

"This isn't really the place a single girl would go to meet guys," he jested.

I giggled. "Actually, I'm meeting someone here."

"Nice. This is a popular place to go on dates," he said. Then he leaned in and continued, with his voice a little lower, "It's more formal than McDonald's, but much more casual than, say, Morton's. The owners claim that everything in

Europe is nicer than here, even casual places."
He rolled his eyes and smiled.

"Is the food good?" I asked.

"I recommend the Salmon Julliard if you like seafood." He winked and wiped the bar with a bar towel.

"Hey, thanks!" I said. I took another sip of my soda and looked around the restaurant.

I could get used to this, I nodded as my thoughts took me to a future of dinners and nice dates with Elmer, the man of my dreams. I pictured our wedding on some far off island - saying our vows under a pergola adorned with wisterias, on the edge of a cliff overlooking the ocean on a breezy, sunny day. I could smell the salty ocean as I took a breath in preparation for the kiss that would seal our eternal matrimony.

"Gracie?" boomed a voice from behind me. My daydream was interrupted by the very man destined to make them come true.

Oh my God, I thought, *he sounds so manly and strong*. I straightened up and squeezed the girls with my elbows to prop them up a little.

They weren't too big, so I had to use as much leverage as possible to seal the deal. Then I turned around, and saw a mustache. A thick, hairy mustache. I didn't even notice the color of his eyes.

"Elmer?" I asked.

"Yes! Nice to finally meet you," he replied. "Let's get a table."

I wanted to ask him about his "subtle" change since he posed for the picture that was on his profile but the chance didn't immediately make itself available because he'd walked away. He was already talking to the hostess. I grabbed my drink and napkin, placed my $200 *Gianet Garçon* clutch under my arm, and followed him.

Our waiter, a skinny young man about twenty years old greeted us at the hostess stand and walked us to our table. After we sat down, the waiter handed us each a menu and said, "I'll be right back to take your drink order." I perused it briefly, then gathered the courage to ask Elmer about his mustache. But again he spoke first.

"So tell me a little bit about yourself."

41

"Uhm, what do you wanna know," I asked.

"Well, where did you grow up, how old are you, ever been married, have kids, that sort of thing," he said, matter-of-factly.

First dates are always so awkward. People never know what to talk about, so they talk about such boring things. I tried to hurry through the small talk. The dim lighting in the restaurant made his mustache look massive, as if it had swallowed his mouth and was inching to consume the rest of his face.

"I grew up here in Fort Lauderdale. Never been married, no kids. You?"

"No marriage, no kids either. So are those stories all true, the ones on your profile?"

"Oh yes. So I take it you didn't search for the videos of me on YouTube, huh," my eyes kept darting back and forth from my soda to his mustache.

"Nah. I'm not really into YouTube. So what did you and that guy talk about during your drive when your car blew up?"

"We were actually silent pretty much the whole way. It felt like an eternity being in that car with him. It was so embarrassing, but people love to hear about it."

"Ha ha, it's actually what made me want to meet you," he said, his mustache waving at me with each word that came out of his mouth.

"There was another story I wanted to put on there, but I decided against it." I started to look through my purse to find something that would distract me from talking to his mustache.

"What was it about?" he asked.

The waiter returned to our table with pen and pad in hand. "Drinks, anyone?" he asked.

"Bourbon. Neat," said Elmer.

"I'll stick with soda. Diet," I said, pointing to my nearly-empty glass.

"Oh, and a round of waters," added Elmer. Our waiter nodded and walked off.

"So what were we talking about?" I asked.

"Another story on your profile?"

"Oh yeah. There was a turtle that crawled into our back yard somehow and my mother wanted me to bring it into the house because she wanted to put it on the console table by the entrance. It's good luck, you know," I started.

He didn't respond, so I continued. "So I walked up to it and it snapped at my foot and held on to my big toe. We had to call the paramedics to try and pry its mouth open and pull my toe out. I was on the news and everything."

"That mustache hurt," he said.

I looked up at him in shock and demanded, "*What* did you say?"

"I said that must've hurt."

"Oh," I said between embarrassed laughter, "I heard something else. So tell me about yourself. What do you do?"

"Well, I actually made quite a bit of money at a casino when I was younger, and rather than stashing it away, I invested it; now I just live off of my dividends."

Oh, you 'stached it alright, buddy, I thought. I took a sip of my soda again and finally gained the courage again to ask him why he hadn't updated his profile picture. Damnit, I was determined to find out the reason behind his deception.

"Wow. So tell me-" but I was then interrupted by the waiter. He placed our drinks and glasses of water in front of each of us, and stepped back with a pen and a pad. He was young, blonde, and the reason this place couldn't be considered "fancy". He tried to be professional at times, but he was still too informal.

"Hey ma'am, are you ready to order?"

"Oh, yes, I'll have the mustache. I mean, the Salmon Julliard." Crap. I didn't think Elmer noticed my little slip-up, because he didn't react at all. But the waiter sure noticed; he raised his eyebrows and smiled at me, nodding. I could only picture Tommy, some pothead kid from high school who used to give me the same look whenever I did something stupid, and he'd say, "Right on!"

"I'll have the duck," said Elmer.

Our young waiter took our menus, and as he walked away he looked back at me and gave me the look again. To avoid laughing, I quickly looked away and back at Elmer, but his eyes again lost my attention to his more pronounced attribute.

Thinking back, he probably thought I was cross-eyed or something because I never took my eyes off that thing. I felt like I was having a date with his upper lip. I didn't know what to do with a guy with a mustache. I was just an innocent Jewish girl from South Florida minding her own business. This is something that *Mother Dearest* should have taught me.

"So what do you do for fun," asked Elmer before taking a sip of water.

The conversation continued about little things: my morning walks, Morgott; his boat, fishing; my love of women's volleyball; his love of dining out; my mother; his sister. I never got the chance to segue into our styling or grooming decisions.

When our food arrived, I was a bit relieved. I was getting a little tired of the small talk. Nothing, however, could prepare me for the onslaught of horrifying images that flew past me like birds fleeing from a storm as I watched him gormandize his duck. Duck flesh on the 'stache. Whiskey on the 'stache. Grain of rice on the 'stache. Chocolate flambè on the 'stache (which I thought would catch on fire, to be honest).

When the duck's fracas with the mustache was over, Elmer wiped his face with his napkin and he was clean as new.

"If you'll excuse me for a moment," he said, getting up to go to the restroom, I supposed.

Thank God it's all over, I thought to myself. *I'll have to change my profile tonight and add "No mustaches need apply".*

When he returned, he paid the check and we stood to leave. *At least he paid*, I thought.

"Let me walk you to your car," he said.

Okay, he wants to be a gentleman, I thought. I politely nodded and walked out.

So he walked me to my car and opened the driver side door for me. We stood awkwardly, and I was trying to avoid looking at him. His hulking figure loomed over me - so close that I could practically see the mustache brushing dust off my *Charmand* shoes. That's when I knew he would try to kiss me, but I couldn't - I didn't know how to kiss a man with a mustache!

Elmer grabbed both of my hands and leaned in like a cat, trying to lift my head with his nose. I tried, I really tried to avoid him but he was so insistent. He squeezed my hands and whispered again, "I had a really good time, and I'd like to see you again." He had brushed his teeth after dinner; I could smell the minty toothpaste on his breath.

I peeked up at him and bit my lip. My eyes slowly returned to his mustache. I swear I saw it swaying in the wind, like tree limbs in the summer. His tongue ran slightly over his lips, and I knew this was the moment. He was going to try to move in, and I didn't want to be rude by turning away.

He inched closer and I cringed. He was so close I could feel his warm breath on my face, and I could see each hair of the bosky fashion statement, perfectly combed, perfectly trimmed to shape, but full and bushy. I quickly closed my eyes tight and pushed my chin forward with my tongue out, and yes - I licked his mustache.

I *licked* it. Twice.

I was mortified; he was in shock. I quickly let his hands go and waved, a pathetic smile across my face, while I plopped down onto the driver's seat of my car.

"Okay, bye," I said as I closed the door. He was still in shock when I drove away. Full of regret, I looked in the rearview mirror and saw Elmer standing there, shoulders slumped in disappointment.

Oh my god. It was probably the most embarrassing thing to happen to me *all month*.

When I got home, I didn't know what to do. *Could my life get any worse? What if he tried to contact me again?* I walked in my house and looked around for anything that would bring me solace, but eventually I just plopped myself face first on my bed. I didn't even take my shoes off. I didn't know whether to block him or send him an apology via email. *Maybe he didn't notice*, I thought. Yeah, right. How could any man not notice a girl *licking his mustache*?

Suddenly I lifted my head up. Jennifer would know what to do! I rolled over and reached for my new clutch, where I found my phone and dialed my best friend.

We'd met in college, and immediately became friends. She was a bit of an outcast like me. She had a Goth looks, with straight black hair, green eyes, and pale skin. It wasn't a purposeful look; she looked like that naturally. She'd lucked out by finding a guy who was exactly her type, a bit edgy in a heavy metal kind of way. He was not my type, but he was very good looking. They'd gotten married as soon as they returned to Fort Lauderdale from college, and now had two kids, so I didn't see her often but we talked all the time.

"How'd it go?" She asked.

"Oh, God. He had a mustache," I said.

"Ok, so?" she replied.

"I licked it."

"Oh. That's not good." Then she laughed. "Why would you do that? What did he say?"

"I don't know why I did it," I said, "I was confused, I don't know how to kiss a guy with a bushy mustache."

"But what did he say?" she pressed.

"Nothing. He was in shock, even as I drove away."

"Gracie, oh my God. Why do these things always happen to you?"

"I don't know. I must have been really bad in my past life. So what should I do?"

"Nothing. Wait and see if he calls you," she suggested.

"And not mention it at all?"

"Like it didn't happen," she replied. "Nazir! Get down from there!" she called to her son.

Nazir was four years old, and had the energy of a triathlete. Her other son, Ezra, was still a newborn but required constant attention from her. She had no choice but to stay at home, and was lucky that her husband earned enough so she wouldn't have to work.

"But how long should I wait?"

"Give it three days. In the meantime, keep exploring your options. And don't worry about it, there are plenty of men out there. I'm sure you'll find one soon."

Soon? I didn't have "soon". I needed one now.

Chapter 3

Friday, October 31

The Routine

Recovering from my horrible date would be a trying task. I was sad, of course, and the dang message reminder on my phone kept beeping as if to torture me about my nonexistent social life.

I felt like Morgott, who was on the couch laying on his back with his mouth open. His teeth made him look like a wild animal, but his tongue, which was hanging out of his mouth and resting on his cheek, made him look dead to anyone who didn't know better. I was determined not to end up a lonely cat lady in my later years, but it's not always up to you.

Things at work were also a little depressing. I worked at Graduate Plastics, a manufacturer of commercial-grade bins. I was the Purchasing Director, responsible for buying the raw material to fill customer orders, and anything else needed at the office. The place was large, but it was mostly the plant that took up acreage. The office was about 1200 square feet, plus Mr. B's office upstairs.

I sat near the receptionist, named Linda. Her day wasn't complete without some greasy, dripping gossip. It was she, in fact, who perpetuated some stories about me with the other employees. Whenever there was a strange odor or sound in the room, she made a huge ordeal about it, covering her nose and mouth with paper towels. Eventually I became the brunt of an ongoing joke with my coworkers, which was humiliating.

The night I had with Elmer aboard the Pequod was still fresh in my mind, and every time I remembered it, it seemed worse. I shifted in my leather office chair from the memory, and the chair squeaked.

"Gracie!" exclaimed Linda. "How many times do we have to ask you to please excuse yourself to the bathroom or go outside when you want to do that?"

"Whatever, Linda. I'm not in the mood," I said, rolling my eyes.

It was Halloween, so she was dressed like a sexy nurse, with her boobs almost completely exposed. It was so inappropriate for work. Damaris was also dressed to kill as a sexy witch. It was as if there was a contest going on for who could look the sluttiest. I was too depressed to dress up, but then again I never really did anything over-the-top. I was in a casual white blouse from Wal-Mart, black trousers from Express, and flats from some mom-and-pop shoe store.

"You know you shouldn't be wearing white after Labor Day," said Linda. "Well, unless your costume is of a tacky office employee."

I rolled my eyes. "I'm not in the mood."

"What's wrong?" Linda asked.

"I had a horrible night. I don't really want to talk about it."

"Ok, whatever. Are you doing anything for Thanksgiving?"

"I don't know yet. I may go to my mother's."

"Why don't you come to ours? My mom is doing the usual buffet at my house. You know how it is. You can bring your mother too if you want."

I have to say that Linda, or rather, her parents, lived a life of luxury. Their house was on a golf course in an exclusive town in Dade County, and looked like a mansion. But I didn't want to deal with her jerk of a father and her drama with her boyfriend. "Nah, I don't really think I wanna do anything so lavish this year," I said.

"Mr. B is coming," she said in a teasing tone.

Our boss, Mr. Braddock, was very wealthy, and very handsome. He was in his 40's, slender, always dressed in a tailored suit and a crisply-pressed shirt, and had one of those faces that refined with age. Linda was having an affair with him. Actually, so was Damaris, our Controller. And Jeannette, the Accounting girl. And they were all married. Well, Linda just had a boyfriend, but it was all the same. They all thought I was after him, too.

"I don't care. I just want to have a quiet Thanksgiving this year."

With that, I realized I had to call my mother to see if that was the reason she was calling me so much. But I wanted to have a date secured for the event before I agreed to go. Even though I still had about a month, I couldn't help but feel the pressure building in the back of my mind. It was almost like a "floater" in the eye – always there, always annoying, and never relenting.

When I left the office that day I went to the gym to let off some steam. Damaris had told me that one of the best places to meet men was at the gym, but in the month I'd been a member all I could find was meatheads who were too in love with themselves to be able to fall in love with anyone else.

Not that I didn't get hit on. Those guys hit on everything that moved. I always made sure to wear my glasses and tie my hair back so they wouldn't pay much attention to me, but it never worked. The minute they saw a girl in a sports bra and second-skin compression shorts or yoga pants, they became like rabid wombats.

I couldn't understand it. I had a flat butt ("longback", they used to call me in college), my boobs were pretty small, and I looked like a dork. Despite all that, the pervs never ceased to surprise me with their gross acts. Because of this, I only went once or twice a week when I felt like I really needed to punish my body. I usually opted to jog around my neighborhood or use the stairs in my apartment building instead.

After completing fifteen minutes on the *Stair Sensei* I moved to the hip abductor/adductor machine. Of course, I forgot to get a towel to place over my lap, and the stupid meatheads immediately swarmed right in front of my machine to watch me open and close my legs - like a bunch of creeps. I was *so* not in the mood. I had to stop before getting much of a workout, so, annoyed, I called it a day. I decided I'd just have to do some squats at home or do another fifteen flights of stairs.

Monday, November 3

The Doomsday Clock

Thanksgiving was quickly approaching, and I still hadn't called my mother back. It would be any day now before she made an appearance at my place. She had a key to my apartment and sometimes stopped by to do my dishes or my laundry.

This time I didn't have to worry about calling her, though, because she beat me to it.

Thump. Thee thump thump.

Thump thum. Thee thee thump.

My cellphone rang with my latest favorite ringtone: a hip hop song by "Mr. C, the Mr. E" titled, "BTY". It was a catchy tune, and an interesting social commentary on thug life, but I was getting sick of it because people called my phone so much. Morgott also seemed to hate it, because he'd run and hide whenever he heard it. This time was no different.

I put my *Larrie Buttoin* knock-off purse on the kitchen counter raked through all my necessities to find my cellphone. Sure enough, it was my mother.

"Yes, mother," I said frantically when I answered.

"Gracie, I've been trying to call you for a month now. What's going on, are you in trouble?"

"No, Mother. I'm fine. I've just been busy, that's all."

"Too busy for your mother? Are you seeing someone?"

"Yes, Mother, I am. So I don't have too much time to dillydally. What's up?"

"Well, I'd like to meet this young man. He is a *young* man, isn't he?"

"Yes, Mother."

"Is he Jewish?"

"No."

"What's his name?"

My thoughts immediately shifted to Elmer's mustache; my tongue gliding over it in slow motion, each hair walking on the surface of my tongue like the legs of a centipede on pavement. It had been four days and he still hadn't called me back.

"You'll meet him once I know we're serious," I said. "Until then, I would appreciate you respecting my privacy."

"I just want to know his name in case I've heard of him or something. Is he rich?"

"See? Why must you do this?"

"I'm just looking out for you, Schumpkin. You need a man that can take care of you. You know that if you're still single by the time you turn thirty, you will never find a man. You'll be single for the rest of your life and everyone will think you're a lesbian. Oh my God, you're not a *lesbian* are you?"

"*Mother*! Of course not! Why would you think that?"

"Well, I don't know. That's very popular with the young people nowadays."

"It's not a *trend*, mother. Never mind. Besides, I told you I'm seeing someone, and yes, it's a man. A young man."

"Did you do a background check on him? You know people nowadays have criminal records and you'd never know it unless you check."

"Right. Is that all you wanted?"

"Well, sweetie I just wanted to invite you to our Thanksgiving dinner. Your Aunt Janice is coming over; you know how she's been since Uncle Mike's passing."

A sinkhole of memories swallowed me up; I was helpless to travel through it.

"Yeah, she's crazier than ever," I mumbled.

"Well, why don't you come over around six and bring your studdly womp so we can meet him."

Crap, I thought. *Now I really put myself in a pickle.*

Chapter 4

End of Freshman Year, High School

The Crazies

Aunt Janice and Uncle Mike were quite the interesting couple. Uncle Mike, my mother's older brother, was in the Air Force stationed in Patrick Air Force Base near Cocoa Beach when he met a Cuban immigrant named Janice Vitali. They had a brief two-month courtship and then got married. Through the years, they moved around like most army families do, and eventually ended up in Tampa, where they finally settled down near MacDill Air Force Base.

The truly interesting thing about Aunt Janice and Uncle Mike was that she didn't speak any English and he didn't speak any Spanish. Visiting them was always an adventure, because they bickered nonstop – each in their respective language. I don't know how they understood each other, but somehow they did. Eventually Aunt Janice learned a few words in English and blended them into her Spanish, creating a new language altogether. When her sisters would visit from Miami, they could barely understand her because of her new language that seemed to have neither rhyme nor reason. Actually, the only ones who could understand her were her kids and Uncle Mike.

Uncle Mike wasn't really all there, either, because he'd argue with my aunt about nonsense. They also did some things that were downright dangerous.

I remember one time we went to visit them in Tampa, and we almost didn't survive the ordeal. My dad had decided that we needed a vacation, so he closed his practice for a week so we could go to Belush Gardens. I hated Belush Gardens back then because there were only like two rides, and the lines were longer than the food lines during the Great Depression. My father refused to stand around for hours to ride anything for less than a minute, so for our family the place was more like a big zoo. My dad, of course, loved it because he could have all the beer he wanted.

So that summer we made the four-hour drive up to Tampa and stayed with my aunt and uncle.

Immediately upon arriving at their house, I knew it was going to be a heck of a week: my cousin Jay, who was a teenager, was having a screaming match with Aunt Janice; my other cousin Lanie, seven years old at the time, was running around the house with my Uncle Mike chasing after her with shoe in hand; and whatever they were cooking in the oven was charred beyond recognition. We didn't even need to see it, because the smell of char was hotly overwhelming, even outside the house.

As we were walking in, my cousin Jay was storming out of the house, and without a word to us he left and didn't come back until the following morning. But eventually everything calmed down at the house and we unloaded our luggage while my Uncle ordered a couple of pizzas.

My parents and I had to sleep in the living room, which I didn't mind except that we had to be up before anyone else. Not that we had a choice: there were no curtains in the living room, so as soon as the sun came up we were bathed in enough sunlight to melt the polar ice caps; then there was my Aunt Janice, who was up at 6:30 every morning to prepare breakfast while she sang songs in Spanglish. With the kitchen right next to the living room, there was no escaping the daily serenade.

If we were lucky enough to sleep through that, though, my Uncle Mike's entrance into the kitchen was sure to do the trick. It was almost immediate; when he entered the kitchen, he and my aunt would start their screaming match.

The breakfast was always odd, too. She would make pancakes and scrambled eggs using infant formula. She always said it was more nutritious than milk. Why she would put milk in scrambled eggs in the first place was beyond me, but she was of the belief that everything – and I mean everything – tasted better when prepared with milk.

In any case, Belush Gardens was exactly what I expected: boring, boring, boring. Well, except for the bit when they shut everything down and locked all the guests in the food court because a disgruntled employee released a bunch of the animals from the reptile exhibit. My father, of course, hung out by the register the entire time, drinking beer after beer.

An hour and a half after being locked into the packed food court, they finally announced, "We appreciate your patience, and you can rest assured the malfunction has been corrected. For the inconvenience, please enjoy ten percent off all purchases at the gift shop. Enjoy the rest of your visit!"

"Oh good," said my mother. "Let's get back on the safari!"

My mother hated to walk and always claimed to have back pain, so wherever we went she wanted to be pushed around on a wheelchair.

"Mother, do I have to push you and those heavy bags the entire time? Can't you roll the wheels yourself for a bit?"

"Maybe your father can push me for a bit," she said.

"Sorry, Mallory," said my father, "I have my hands full." Yeah, he had a beer in each hand, and he could hardly walk as it was.

So I got stuck pushing her massive butt around the entire 500-acre (or whatever) park. One of the two large bags she had with her were packed with food and a change of clothes for each of us in case it rained, and the other was for souvenirs. Mind you, she always thought the souvenirs were too expensive, so we never bought any. Ever.

My back and legs were so sore at the end of the day that I was glad to finally get back to the car and rest during the drive back to my aunt and uncle's house, which was about forty-five minutes. My mother didn't even realize my father was drunk, so she let him drive and we sang merry songs on the whole drive back because my father insisted on it.

When we arrived at my aunt and uncle's house my mother unloaded the two bags she had brought along to the park and set them next to the couch where we were going to sleep.

"Comer and eating las dinner," called my Aunt Janice once we were settled in. She had made some lettuce-wrapped olives with meat sauce – the type you'd put on spaghetti. It was so gross. My dad doesn't know how lucky he was to have passed out as soon as he hit the couch.

My mother and I sat down to eat while my aunt cleaned up the cookware. My uncle was outside, chain-smoking. He always did that when he and my aunt got into a serious fight.

"Si you quieren soda o juice hay plenty in the frideder," she said. I looked at my mom, who was smiling.

"That's so sweet," my mother said. I knew she didn't understand a word.

"How was Belush Garden?" asked my aunt.

"It was ok," I replied.

"Oh my God," said my mother. "All of the animals escaped and attacked us!"

"You kiddie!" said my aunt.

"Mother, they didn't attack us, the staff quarantined us in the food court."

"Yes they did attack us. That lizard was coming straight for us! It had devil eyes, and that tongue! Oh my God, I think it could smell my fear."

I rolled my eyes. Whatever, I figured I'd let her have that fantasy adventure this one time. Better than accepting her husband was so out of it he couldn't even protect his sobriety.

"When you finis just putten the play in the triturator," she said, pointing to the sink.

I nodded. "Is there anything to drink?"

My aunt replied, "In the frideder."

Ah. I got myself a bottled water and one for my mother.

"Ha you see the Walter and Paola?" asked my aunt.

"We saw them a few months ago. I think we might invite them to a barbecue next month," said my mother. I had no clue how she understood my aunt's question.

"Ay, Meeken and me saw both them at the crusero two month ago," said my aunt. "He shit on her in fron everybody," she said.

"What?" I said, in shock. "On the cruise?"

"Yeh. He didn't care who watching him. He shit on her ahi in the pool and in the restaurant of the crusero."

I couldn't imagine a guy doing that to his wife in front of people. I stood up and went to scrape my scraps into the garbage, when my aunt stopped me and said, "No throw here in the triturator." She pointed at the sink.

I had no clue what she said, but I followed her directions and placed everything in the sink.

After clean-up we went back to the living room to watch some awards show. My dad's snoring was so loud we had to put the TV almost on maximum volume.

Almost immediately, my uncle peeked inside the house and yelled, "Janice, would you lower that crap? The neighbors are going to complain!"

Smiling, my aunt lowered the volume and then went to the kitchen. She returned with a glass in hand.

"I bringing you some watte. Es bueno para la salud. You health," she said, placing the glass of water on the end table next to me.

"Thank you," I said. She sat back down next to me to watch the show, and I was sure she had no clue who any of the celebrities were.

"Oh my God," I said to myself, "Ice Cube has lost weight. He looks so good."

"That's por el Global Warning. Caricatur con el ice eeh los pampitos."

I looked, wide-eyed, at my aunt sitting next to me, then I turned toward my mother, who was just coming out of the kitchen.

"Mom, she's talking to me!" I whispered in a panic.

Before she could save me from my aunt's unintelligible conversation, my mother screamed in a panic and jumped back into the kitchen. I looked around to try and see what was causing her to freak out, and Aunt Janice was still talking and laughing as if nothing was happening around her.

"Y entonces I grabbe las tazas con my han eeh I droppe," she said, then laughed, slapping her hands on her thighs.

Suddenly I spotted it. Three snakes slithered around the couch where my aunt and I were sitting. They must have snuck into my mother's bags at Belush Gardens during the sabotage attack. How could they release us from quarantine before accounting for all the escaped animals?

Eventually my aunt spotted them too and reached for the glass of water she had brought me and hurled it at the snakes. Immediately, the creatures went on the offensive, and two of them managed to strike me on my legs, leaving me bloody and stricken with mortal rigor.

"Aaaah!" screamed my aunt. "Meeken, bringi fire!"

"Fire? Are you crazy Janice?" my uncle said as he ran past us and into the kitchen. He returned with a shotgun in hand and aimed it at the snakes near my feet.

"Uncle Mike! Are you crazy?" I shrieked. I don't know if he even understood what I'd said I was screeching so loud.

I kicked my legs up and he fired almost point blank at them. As soon as the shotgun blasted, my father woke up, startled, with his hands in "karate chop" position.

When it was all over, my uncle refused to take me to the hospital. He said they were not venomous snakes, and with his military first aid training he bandaged me up and sent me to walk (or rather, hobble) around the house.

I didn't sleep that night, or for the rest of our "vacation", because I was worried. Not that there'd be more snakes, but that there would be another menace that would spur my uncle to brandish a firearm.

I remember calling Herbie from the phone in the kitchen when everyone was asleep.

"Hey, sorry I can't talk long, this is costing my aunt and uncle," I said when he answered.

"How's the vacation going?"

"Ugh. I got attacked by three snakes, and my uncle almost shot me with a shotgun."

"What?"

"Yeah, but I'm ok. I can't wait to get back home."

"It'll be over before you know it, Grace," he reassured me.

"I know. And if I never see another reptile or gun again I'd die a happy girl."

Wednesday, November 5

The Rat and the Snake

When I checked my computer in the morning I saw that another guy had contacted me. His name was Eddie, and he was pretty hot. In his picture he looked a bit like a frat boy, but with kind features: round eyes, groomed short blonde hair, and clothes that didn't seem too pretentious; he wore jeans, a button-down with rolled-up sleeves, and trendy brown and white sneakers.

On his profile he said he loved animals, which I thought would make him very compatible with me and my family, and he also mentioned that whoever he dated had to accept his routine, which included speaking with his parents at least three times per week.

His message was short and very sweet:

Hi Gracie:

I would love to take you out sometime. You sound like a really cool, down to earth kind of person. And I'd LOVE to meet Morgott.

I replied to his email immediately.

Hi Eddie, you sound like a perfect match for me. I'd like to get together sooner than later. When are you available?

I sent out the email with fingers crossed. He replied rather quickly with his phone number and asked for mine. I called him from work.

"Hey!" he said when he answered. "I'm so glad you called."

"How are you?" I said.

"Oh, great! Just hanging out, you know. Hey, so what's the deal with 'sooner than later'?"

"Nothing. I've just been strung along by a bunch of guys on the website," I lied.

"Idiots. I promise I won't do that to you. Are you free tonight?"

I was taken aback. I wanted soon, but I didn't expect to be going on a date that very night. "Uh, sure. What do you have in mind?"

"How 'bout I make dinner and we watch a movie at my place? I think it would be a great way to get to know each other."

Sure. Relaxed atmosphere, no pretension. "As long as you don't give me food poisoning, I'm ok with that," I said.

So it was set, and I'd be meeting him outside his apartment building at 6:30. I had Jennifer on alert, and my cell phone handy in case I needed an escape or if he turned psycho.

He lived out west in Lauderhill, in a rather old-looking apartment building. I don't like to judge people by where they live - God knows I've lived in pretty crappy places before - but this place looked like the friggin' projects.

When he came downstairs I was glad to see he was normal. The only thing that bothered me about him was that he came downstairs wearing shorts and was barefoot, which I couldn't imagine ever doing, especially in this dirty place. But at least he didn't have a mustache.

"Oh my God," I said when I saw him, "you look just like your picture."

"So do you," he said. "Why is that a surprise?"

"Never mind," I said.

He gave me a hug, grabbed my hand, and walked me to the elevator. He pressed number four and smiled at me. I smiled back, but as soon as I looked down at the floor my smile faded. The floor of the elevator looked like someone had spilled an entire six-pack of beer on it, and his toes were filthy.

"You're gonna love my roommates," he said when the elevator stopped. *Roommates*?

Eddie led me into the apartment he apparently shared with three other guys. He told me that they would all be there, but that they were a lot of fun to hang out with and that I would like them. I figured there'd be nothing wrong with watching a movie and having a good time with his friends.

Inside, the apartment's condition should have been no surprise, it being a bachelor pad and all, but I was aghast at the amount of trash on the floor. It reminded me about my own apartment and how I needed to clean up a little in case I ever had a date over. Well, not clean - because I was never dirty - but pick up.

The smell in Eddie's apartment was that of old, rotting food mixed with the smell of weed; there were empty pizza boxes, buckets with chicken bones in them, and boxes of old fried rice that seemed to be crawling to life from some Chinese take-out on the floor. Full garbage bags sat by the main entrance.

I forced a smile and tried to avoid stepping on anything that might be alive in the numerous food containers that decorated the floor.

"Hey Eddie. Who's the chick?" asked one of the guys who was sitting on the floor in front of the couch playing on his Playstation. The other two guys were zoned out, sitting on the couch, staring at the TV screen. I figured they were high.

"This is Gracie," replied Eddie.

"Gracie, this is Frank. That's Yolek, and that bum over there is Larry."

"Hi guys," I said, holding an open hand to my shoulder.

"Hey, you want something to drink?" asked Eddie. "We have beer, soda, whatever."

"I'll have a Diet Coke," I replied.

"Sit, sit," he said, shoving Yolek and Larry to make a space for me in the center of the couch. When I sat down the two simply stared at me like zombies. I felt so awkward that all I could do was adjust my skirt and say "hi" again. I must have saluted them three times.

Finally Eddie returned with a can of Coke. "We don't have diet," he said, handing me the can.

"That's okay, thanks," I said.

"So," said Larry in slow motion, "how do you know Eddie?"

"We met through a dating site," I replied.

Eddie, who was standing next to the TV facing us, smiled and raised his eyebrows at Larry. I must say I didn't like that; it looked kind of creepy, as if he was signaling to his friends that he'd won some kind of contest.

"So all of you live here?" I segued.

"Yeah, like," said Larry as if trying to find words in an alphabet soup. "Sometimes we like, go there, and then we chill here."

I looked at Eddie and opened my eyes wide, trying to signal to him that I was not comfortable sitting there with those guys. Thankfully he got the message.

"Uh, Gracie. Why don't we go to my room? I don't have a TV in there or anything but maybe we could finger paint or something."

Whatever. It was a way out. I stood and followed Eddie toward his room, but we never reached it. On the way there, I spotted what looked like a huge bald rat crawling on the floor just outside the hallway that led to the bedrooms. I immediately let out a scream that could bring Frankenstein's monster to life and ran back to the couch, trampling Frank and Larry. Yolek was still in a trance, so I don't think he even noticed.

"Oww," said Larry, who then lifted his hand to rub his arm where I had stepped on him. When he did that, he bumped me off the back of the couch, so I frantically got up and ran toward the dining room and climbed up on the glass table. I was wailing the entire time, like an ambulance hurtling toward a hospital with a patient who was both convulsing into a seizure and having a coronary, and Eddie was trying frantically to diffuse the situation.

"Wait, wait, Gracie! It's ok, it's ok," he kept saying.

"There's a freakin' rat! A rat!" I shrieked.

"Wait, no, it's a mouse- look. He's food," he tried to explain.

"What? You eat rats?" I was still stomping my feet on the glass table, just in case the thing crawled up on it and onto my pant legs.

"No," he said, now noticeably getting frustrated. "He's food for-" but he couldn't finish. He didn't need to, as the situation went from worst to worstest.

The mouse was crawling toward the dining room table where I was, and out of nowhere what must have been an Anaconda leaped out and snatched the mouse, then crawled under the dining table and, as if to horrify me to my wit's end, sat there for me to watch in delirium as it swallowed the rodent whole. I don't think I screamed harder in my entire life, and I think it was the screams that were responsible for the next incident.

I stomped and screamed while the shape of the rodent made its way through the body of the ophidian horror, and then, out of nowhere, the glass tabletop shattered and I fell through, right on top of the hellish creature. I don't remember anything else, except that I woke up about an hour later on the filthy floor outside Eddie's apartment building.

Eddie was nowhere to be found, and the EMT's that were working on me when I awoke told me they had received a call about a homeless woman passed out and possibly injured on the sidewalk.

I don't know if I walked downstairs on my own or if the guys brought me down to avoid being caught with marijuana and then called the emergency number; but in the end, I think I killed their snake. At the very least I broke their dining room table, so I never called again.

My one-night stay at the hospital was beyond humiliating. The doctors had to pull shards of glass from my back and butt.

I was with a nurse when my hospital phone rang.

"Oh my God," whimpered my mother on the other end of the phone, "my poor Baumscheeks!"

"Mother, I'm fine. I just have a few scratches," I kept saying to try and calm her down.

"A few scratches! You are delicate and you need a doctor there with you at all times. When I was there earlier they only had one nurse there with you."

"Wait, you were here? At the hospital?" I asked.

"Of course I was there, Schumpkin! I had to see you!"

I could only imagine what type of embarrassment she'd left in her wake.

"Put the doctor on immediately. Oh God, oh God, what have I done for this to happen to my Schumpkin?"

I looked at the heavyset nurse, who was dark skinned; maybe Hispanic. Her name was Larissa.

"Larissa, please please please tell her you're a doctor," I begged, my hand covering the microphone on the handset.

"Gracie, I'm not allowed to do that. I just recently passed my board exam, and impersonating a doctor could get me in big trouble," she said, refusing to take the phone.

"Please, you don't understand," I said.

"I'm sorry. I'll page the doctor." She walked out of the room, and I could hear her paging the doc.

Once my mother was off the phone and Larissa was back in my room, I set out to get details about my mother's visit.

"Were you on duty when my mother stopped by?" I asked.

"Yes, why?" she said, trying to hide her smirk.

"Please tell me she behaved herself."

"Well, it was like an ancient Greek play - full of drama. She acted like you were on your deathbed."

"What do did she do?" I pressed.

"Well, if you've seen that movie 'The Omen', she was screaming and crying like if you were the priest that got impaled outside the church. She refused to sign any paperwork without a lawyer present to review it first, as if the hospital was asking for her permission to pull the plug on you. It was kind of cute. She really cares about you."

"Oh no," I said, covering my face with my hands.

Larissa continued. "She also demanded emergency surgery, painkillers, two nurses to care for you bedside 24 hours per day, and a doctor nearby at all times too."

"Oh, God."

"Oh, and, because she wouldn't let up, we had to stage a private room for you with a doctor and two nurses. It was the only way to get her to go home for the night."

"Please tell me that was it," I said, reaching behind me for the pillow so I could cover my face with it.

"Nah. That's it!" she said with a smile. "Now get some rest, you'll be out of here in the morning."

I'm sure Larissa was there more to approve my discharge the minute I was eligible, rather than to make sure my "condition" didn't worsen.

I spent the night praying that they'd release me first thing in the morning before my mother could visit again and put on another show. At night I could barely sleep, and all I could hear from the hallway was the night nurses talking about me and my mother.

She thought Doctor Jimenez was the janitor!

Oh my God, I know. Then she told Doctor Greenbaum to get the doctor! She couldn't believe that Doctor Greenbaum was just as qualified as a male doctor.

*And how about the daughter? I heard they
found her passed out in an alley somewhere.
And did you see her clothes? Filthy!*

I was completely humiliated, and I couldn't run from it.

But worst of all, I still had no date for Thanksgiving.

Sophomore Year, High School

The Death of Bones

Bones was a good cat. Her coat was black and white, but not like a zebra; the white patches were shaped like bones. And she was so loving and cuddly; I loved her more than anything growing up. She loved to rub up against my skin and sit on my lap. Often she'd bring a toy and drop it at my feet so I could play with her. Of course, like with everything else, my mother ruined that joy for me.

It was a particularly hot summer here in South Florida; we'd had a lot of rain early in the summer, so it was very humid and muggy. The birds and butterflies loved it, and the iguanas sunbathed daily on the safety rails next to the canals. I remember the day that we decided to have a cookout in the backyard, and my mother and father had some friends over, Walter and Paola. They brought their son Herbie with them.

I was sixteen, so I had nothing in common with my parents' friends, so Herbie and I just played with Bones in the yard. We played "chase the mouse" for a while and had a great time. My dad was grilling burgers and kosher dogs; ah, the smell of summer. My mother was in the kitchen preparing the condiments, slicing tomatoes, and chopping lettuce. She was watching everything that went on outside with a keen eye, as always.

My dad sipped his beer while he grilled the meats and told his friends stories from his college days at Dartmouth; his friends just laughed along.

When my father finished his beer, he leaned into the cooler to get another but he was all out. I didn't want to stick around and have to be an accomplice in getting him drunk, so I walked inside the house to look for another toy for with Bones.

"He's having an affair, you know," said my mother to my father when he went inside to get more beers out of the fridge. I was in the living room combing for Bones's other toys.

"Who?" asked my father.

"Walter. He's sleeping with Miriam," she continued.

"Now why would you start such nasty rumors, Mallory?"

"It's not a rumor. I know it. Miriam told me, and Janice saw them on the cruise," replied my mother.

"Well, it doesn't matter. That's their business, not ours," replied my father.

"It *is* our business. He's a cheater."

Little did my mother know at this point that my father was having an affair of his own. In fact, he was seeing Miriam, too. But even worse, he was also seeing Walter's wife, Paola.

Whenever my mother went to the grocery store, he would call one of them over. He would tell me that whoever it was that came over had a concern about some growth on her back so he had to examine her in private. It would seem to the untrained eye like there was something going around. I knew better, though. It was only a matter of time before my mother found out, too.

"I don't see how the fact that he's a cheater is our business," said my father.

"He brings a bad influence to this house. And his poor wife. I feel like having her stay here for a few weeks until they get a divorce."

"They're not getting a divorce, Mallory," replied my father. And as much as he probably wanted Paola to stay with us for a few weeks, he knew better. It would be too risky to do it right under my mother's nose.

"They will, once she finds out. And she will find out. Mark my words," said my mother, holding her index finger in the air.

I had found Bones's toy and I stood at the entryway of the kitchen, waiting for my parents to finish talking so I could cross through to the backyard. When they saw me standing there, my parents suddenly got quiet.

I shrugged my shoulders and crossed through to the backyard. My parents just stood in an awkward silence.

I didn't care to take part in adult drama, so I waved it off and called out for my cat.

"Bones! I have your favorite toy!"

But she didn't come, which was weird because she usually ran toward me when I offered her the toy.

"Bonesy! I have your favorite toy!"

There was still no response. I looked around the yard, but I couldn't find her. Then I heard Paola scream, and I ran in her direction. Bones was a few feet from her. She had apparently tried to crawl toward her and Walter, but she stopped short, falling on her side. She was having a heatstroke or something. Herbie hadn't noticed because he was stuffing his fat face with burgers and kosher dogs.

I screamed in horror, and when he saw how frantic I was, Herbie stuffed the last of his burgers in his mouth and ran to help me, with crumbs, ketchup, and mustard rolling down his face with his saliva.

"Let's take her inside," said Herbie, rushing to open the door for me.

I picked Bones up and ran inside to tell my mother to help her. "Please mommy, do something!"

"Don't worry sweetheart," she said before shuffling to her bedroom. When she returned, she had what looked like a pen in hand. "I always have a couple of Epi Pens on hand in case of emergency. Lay her down here on the counter."

Now, my dad was a doctor. He knew about this stuff, but he was just not around enough to use his skills on us or our pets. This time, he happened to be in the bathroom when the emergency arose. So my mother took it upon herself to remedy the situation with her wonderful expertise. She uncapped the pen, raised it above her shoulder, and stabbed Bones in the chest with it. Herbie and I just stared blankly during the procedure.

"Now give her about a minute and she'll be like new," said my mother as she withdrew the syringe pen.

Bones had a convulsion immediately after my mother administered the medication, but my mother told me that was normal. A minute passed. Then two. On the twelfth minute, my father came out of the bathroom. I was bawling.

"What's going on," he asked.

"I can't imagine why it didn't work," said my mother, handing the Epi Pen to my father.

"Mallory, what did you do? What happened?" He demanded.

"She had a heatstroke, so I gave her the Epi," said my mother, matter-of-factly.

My dad let out an exasperated breath. "Mallory, when any creature goes into heatstroke, their blood pressure drops and their heart races. If you give her epinephrine, you're sending her heart into overdrive. She needed fluids, not stimulants. This," he held up the Epi Pen, "is for anaphylaxis. Allergies. Bones is dead."

"Nooooo!" I cried out. Herbie immediately hugged me tightly.

"Oh my," said my mother. "Well, now I know."

"*Now you know*?" I was crying so hard I could barely speak. "Mother, you killed our cat! You killed *Bones*!"

"Well, better her than you. Be glad it wasn't you having that heatstroke. God knows why he does things."

"What are you saying?" I demanded.

"Mallory, stop," said my father. "You're not helping."

"What? I'm just saying that obviously God wanted Bones with Him. That's ok, your father and I will get you two new cats and before you know it you'll forget all about Bones," she said.

Yeah, she got two cats: East and West. But they were not for me. They took care of her when my father left her, and I was left to mourn Bones by myself. I cried every night for a month, and I didn't leave my room, only to go to school.

Saturday, November 8

The Escape

Thump. Thee thump thump.

Thump thum. Thee thee thump.

My mother was calling again. She always seemed to know when I was walking through the door. I hurried inside and retrieved my cellphone from my purse.

"Hello?" I said, answering the phone.

"Sweetie, I need a huge favor," she said.

"What is it, mother?"

"I have to go pick up your Aunt Janice at the airport, but I need to get East out of the groomer's. Can you go pick him up for me?"

"Sure, mother. At what time will he be ready?"

"At two. And make sure to ask them if they cleaned out his boombie. He was really smelling like something died down there."

"Oh my God, Mother! Why do you always have to make me do these embarrassing things? Do I really have to ask them that? Is it really necessary?"

"Of course! I don't want to have East sitting on my shoulder smelling like the cat from *Cujo*."

"It's *Pet Sematary*. Cujo was a dog."

"Whatever. It's important that you do this for me today, okay, Schumpkin?"

"Ok, fine. I'll do it. Do I have to pay anything?"

"No, it's all paid for already, sweetheart," she said.

"Ok, it's one o'clock. I gotta go take a shower right now to make it by two."

"Thank you, I love you, Schumpkin!"

"Sure, love you too, bye."

After I hung up, I called for Morgott to sit on the couch with me for a moment. When he didn't immediately come over, I looked around the apartment and saw that in my rush to get in the house and answer my mother's call, I had left the front door ajar.

Morgott was nowhere to be found.

Chapter 5

Senior Year, High School

The Ünguent

The cutest boy in school had asked me out, and I was excited to make him my first boyfriend. His name was Memphis, and he had curly blonde hair, was athletic, and he wore the coolest, trendiest clothes. He was a skater who made his own rules, and seemed to have a deep understanding of the world around him. Every girl wanted to date him. Enter October.

October was the Captain of the volleyball team, and she was the female version of Memphis. All the boys wanted her, but her heart was taken. She'd dated Memphis the year before, but he broke up with her because she was too jealous. Needless to say, the rejection made her want him even more, so she did not allow anyone to date him.

Memphis walked into our volleyball practice after school one day, and straight up to me. I was feeling self-conscious, being so sweaty, but when I realized what he was doing, I completely forgot all about that.

"Hey Gracie," he said, without looking at any of the other girls on my team. "Let's go out on Saturday. Seven o'clock."

"Uhm, O.K.," was all I could say in response.

When October saw Memphis ask me out, I knew it would be war. I had to prepare myself. I had to plan a defensive for when she struck. But she apparently didn't need to plan, because she started her attack immediately. While Memphis was talking to me, she was talking with Monica loudly, so both Memphis and I could hear.

"She's so gross. I don't think she ever wears deodorant. You know she doesn't brush her teeth. She chews on grass instead!"

They both laughed. I just rolled my eyes.

"So it's a date," said Memphis.

"Sure," I replied.

"Wear something cute, not your volleyball uniform," he said.

I looked down at my outfit and smiled in embarrassment. I pulled my shirt down to cover my body. He ignored my embarrassment and simply said, "See you Saturday." He was so cool.

Then, as soon as Memphis left, October called out, "Ok, teams, switch! Tammy, Jodie, Susan, Carrie, and Gracie. You'll be South Court. Ines, Ruth, Monica, Jessie, and me will be on North Court."

We arranged ourselves into position for a new game, and on the first serve October slammed the ball in my face.

"Oww!" I screamed.

"Don't be such a baby, Grazer," said October.

I held my lip and saw I was bleeding. I menacingly squinted my eyes at her. She thought she was so cute with her blonde ponytail and her big boobs. "You did that on purpose!"

"First, it's a game, and second, you should have blocked," she said, matter-of-factly. Then she turned around and high-fived her best friend Monica. Ugh.

The next serve, she called the return again, and again she slammed me - this time in the chest, almost knocking me to the floor, and knocking all the wind out of me.

"Ok, that's it," I said. I stormed back to the locker room, changed, and called my mother to pick me up. I didn't go to practice the rest of the week, just in case October had plans of serving some more sabotage.

On Saturday, however, it wasn't October who worried me. I woke up with a massive pimple on my upper lip. It looked like a cold sore, and I was worried that it would still look like that when I met with Memphis. Still young and naïve, I went to my mother for advice.

"Mother, I look like a diseased monster!"

"Oh, honey, it's not that bad," she replied. "You look delicate as always."

"Oh *cut* it mother. Don't tell me you can't see the huge Mount Everest-sized zit on my upper lip."

"Don't worry about that, sweetie. That'll be gone by seven o'clock. Here, let me get you the special ünguent."

"The special what?

"Ünguent. It's an ointment with special herbs and medicines to help get rid of acne pimples," she said.

Who was I to argue?

She retrieved a small tube from the bathroom. It was labeled *Preparation H*. I had no clue what it was.

"Close your eyes, honey," she said. She proceeded to empty the entire tube on my face. Almost immediately, my face felt tingly, then went numb.

"Is this supposed to numb me, mother?" I asked.

"Yes, just leave it on for about an hour and you'll be good as new."

I believed her. I trusted her. And amazingly, she was right. It worked. The pimple was almost completely gone by the time I had to start getting ready for my big date. I was ecstatic.

"Thank you thank you thank you," I said, hugging and kissing my mother.

She smiled and said, "It's no problem, honey. You know I'll do anything for my little Schumpkin." She gave me a kiss and said, "Now go get ready so you're not late for the movie."

I took a shower, put on my trendiest ripped jeans and off-shoulder t-shirt, got my makeup going, and blow-dried my hair so that it was as straight as the hands on a clock. At seven o'clock exactly, Memphis was at the door.

My mother let him in and offered him something to drink. She was behaving herself perfectly! I came out and Memphis and I kissed each other on the cheek, then my mother said, "Remember her curfew is ten o'clock!" To which Memphis replied, "Don't you worry, Mrs. Feldman. We'll be back on time."

We walked outside and I saw he had borrowed his brother's convertible Mustang. It was a dreamy car: red, with white racing stripes, and tan leather seats.

I immediately pictured me and Memphis cruising through the beach with the top down, the wind playing with my hair. I imagined us having a fifth floor condo right on the water, where we could look out the window, which of course took up the entire east wall and captured the view of the ocean better than Aivazovsky. I imagined yachts by the beach, and of course, the biggest one would be ours so we could enjoy it even from our condo.

"So how was your day," interrupted Memphis.

I giggled. "You're not going to believe it, but I almost canceled on you."

"Whoa. How come?"

"Well," I began, "I woke up with the biggest zit right on my upper lip."

He looked over at me. "Wow, you can't even tell. What'd you do?"

"My mom gave me some of her special ünguent to get rid of it," I said. His eyes were round and large; I could tell he was interested in learning a lot from me, and I was interested in teaching him.

"What's an ünguent?" he asked.

"It's like an ointment for pimples - duh! It's called *Preparation H*. 'H' for 'Happiness'."

He shot a wide-eyed look at me, his eyes practically taking up his entire face, and pulled over into the first parking lot we came to.

"What did you say?" he demanded.

"The ünguent for pimples. It's called *Preparation H*. Works like a charm," I said, waving both thumbs in a celebratory way.

"Yagh!" he gagged. He then spat out the window several times. "Grazer Feldman, you are as sick as they say!"

I was confused.

"What?" I asked.

"'Preparation H' is a hemorrhoid cream. You put *ass cream* all over your face and I kissed you on your cheek! Get out. Call your mom to pick you up, and don't call me. Like, ever." He continued to wipe his tongue on his sleeve.

"But," I began, "it wasn't me, it was..."

It was too late for me, that's what it was. He had picked up his phone and dialed.

"Hey. Whatchu doin' tonight?" he said on the phone, all the while staring at me, waiting until I exited the vehicle.

I tried to look as pathetic as possible, hoping to get a pity save, but it was no use. He was already having a full conversation with *her*.

"Nah, didn't work out. I realized you were a better catch," he said. Then I closed the door in shame and stood in the breezy Fort Lauderdale night, under the condescending Fort Lauderdale moon.

He ended up going back to October that night, but they didn't last a week.

When my mother came to pick me up, Herbie was in the car with her. She'd called him and picked him up when she heard how distraught I was.

It was very thoughtful of her, because I knew I could always count on him to listen to my horror stories. If he wasn't fat and gay, he'd be a great catch for any girl. And the poor kid; his parents were going through divorce proceedings. Paola had found out that Walter had been cheating on her and immediately demanded a divorce. She was trying to take everything. But Walter wasn't stupid; he hired a private detective and found out she was also having an affair, although the investigator was never able to identify her lover – he was always in disguise if they met in public, or he'd have her picked up by taxi and brought to our house via boat so that she couldn't be followed.

I got in the car and tried to hold back my tears.

"Wow, Gracie," said Herbie to me on the drive home. "I'm sorry you had to go through that. I can't believe he'd just dump you in the middle of nowhere like that."

"Well, at least my Schumpkin is safe," chimed my mother.

"Thanks for coming, Herbie," I said. "I really need someone to talk to right now. This was so humiliating."

He looked back and gave me the most gentle, reassuring smile. His dimpled cheeks made him so adorable.

Herbie always dressed in a short-sleeved button-down and khakis up to his waist, like a doll. But he never stood a chance in high school. Never mind that he was immensely fat, he was also always in the boys' locker room or trying to join some sports team – which got him teased even more about his sexual orientation, even though he vehemently denied being gay.

"How about we all go for ice cream?" my mother asked us.

I looked at Herbie and we both smiled. She definitely knew our weakness in times of trouble.

"Yay!" we both cheered. Suddenly things didn't seem so bad.

Sunday, November 9

The Pig With a Pig

I woke up on Sunday with a huge zit on my face. I hadn't had a pimple since high school, but I guess all the stress of losing Morgott and the looming Thanksgiving dinner with my mother was catching up to me. After I brushed my teeth I opened my medicine cabinet and stared at the tube of *Preparation H*. An army of memories marched into my head, led by the Noyans of Nostalgia: Memphis, October, and Herbie. I hadn't seen any of them since college graduation.

I coated my face and while I waited for the meds to do their trick I served myself breakfast and checked my email to see if anyone had posted anything about Morgott on the community Bulletin Board. Nobody had even read my post from the day before. Figures; the old Jewish ladies had better things to do than go on the internet. Not that they'd even know how to use it.

I typed up a quick "Missing" flyer and set it to print, then sat down on the couch and watched some TV. The Food Channel was playing a marathon of "Drive-ins, Dives, and Diners" featuring Dude Ferro; it was one of my favorite shows.

When two hours had passed I decided it was time to take a shower. If any guy knew I used "Tail n' Mane" horse shampoo to tame my thick Jewish hair they'd probably run faster than Memphis did; but like with the ünguent, my mother recommended this shampoo and it actually worked really well. But I wasn't going to reveal that secret to any guy, no matter how well we got along or how long we knew each other.

My house was still a mess, but I was not going to have time to clean up that weekend because this focus group was going to pay me $300 for an hour of my time to analyze some products for market; they were paying me to give my honest consumer opinion about them. I had to be in downtown at noon. My boss Mr. Braddock had offered me the opportunity, because it was a friend of his who owned the market research company and he always needed people to do these focus groups. This was going to be the easiest $300 I ever made.

Before I left I flipped through the stack of "Missing" posters I'd just printed. I thought I'd have more luck finding Morgott if I posted them throughout the neighborhood, rather than give them out to individuals. But being that he was so lazy and likely never actually left the apartment building, I had a stack just for my neighbors. He had never run away before, but maybe him seeing me so stressed-out spooked him a little.

I grabbed about half the stack and went through all six floors of my building, leaving a poster in front of each apartment door.

Noon was fast approaching and I still had to get downtown, so I'd have to post the neighborhood flyers after I returned from the focus group.

I always liked downtown Fort Lauderdale because it had that Manhattan feel without making you feel overpowered by too many large buildings. Plus, since it was near the beach, there was always a nice breeze blowing in the area.

This particular building where the focus group was going to meet was seven stories of glass on the outside, and once I entered, I was overwhelmed by the high ceiling that featured some paintings *a la* Sistine Chapel. The reception desk was large, made of cherry oak with a marble top, and the receptionist was a pretty, young redhead who blended in well with the dècor. So after she took down my name, she directed me to the waiting room where several other participants were already sitting.

Thirty of us sat there for several minutes, and then a guy who looked homeless walked in the room with a file in hand.

"Hi, everyone, my name is Bárton, but you can call me Barry," he said with a French accent. "I will be conducting this focus group. Please follow me to the focus room."

He led us through the hall down to the last room, where there was a huge conference table with chairs all around it. It easily fit all thirty of us, and still had room for Barry and nine others.

"Please have a seat and we'll begin," he said.

I sat down next to a brown-haired guy with a beard who was about forty-five and had a heavy Spanish accent. He was slightly above medium build, dressed in a short-sleeve button down, slacks, and dress shoes. He wore glasses that made him very approachable.

"Hi, I'm Gracie," I said, extending my hand.

He shook it, then kissed it. "Rigoberto," he said.

I felt it was a bit weird for him to kiss my hand, but I figured it was a cultural thing.

"Where are you from, Rigoberto?" I asked.

"Me? I'm Cuban." He was loud, I should have guessed he was Cuban.

"Oh. Surprise there, huh?"

He smiled.

"Our first product is called the 'Spectafier'," said Barry, interrupting me and my new friend, and officially beginning the group.

He demonstrated the product, which was a baby's pacifier with looped legs attached to each side, like glasses.

"I will play a short video," he said, "then you can all look at the prototype closer and take notes."

The video featured several mothers holding babies in a doctor's office waiting room. The mothers talked about how impossible it was to keep the pacifiers in their babies' mouths and how expensive it was becoming to have to buy new pacifiers every few weeks.

"Well, those days are over - introducing the 'Spectafier'," said the announcer in the video, which was like a 'Spotted on TV' infomercial.

The product was billed as a pacifier that was guaranteed not to fall out of the baby's mouth and had no risk of strangulation. I thought it was a pretty good idea. I didn't have any kids, so I didn't even know this was a problem. In the movies they always make it look like it's hard for a baby to lose its pacifier once it's in its mouth.

When the video was over, Barry passed out a form for us to fill out with our comments and evaluation. I rated the product a 4 out of 5 because it was so darn ugly and because it had a terrible name, but it was apparently a good product.

Barry then brought out the next product, called the "Mud Tracker". It was a small GPS chip that could be implanted under the sole of a shoe. It was useful in tracking kids, elderly loved ones, or a spouse suspected of cheating. Rigoberto immediately scoffed at the product.

"What a useless piece of crap," he said.

Barry paused the video. "Why do you say that?" he asked.

"Because, my wife want to put one of those in all my shoes."

I looked over at him.

"Are you cheating on her?" asked Barry.

"She always accusing me when she have no proof," he replied.

Barry smiled. "Oh. But *are* you cheating on her?"

"Yeah, I cheated on her but why she accuse me when she have no proof?"

Everyone in the room laughed.

"How dare she," I said with a smile.

Rigoberto looked at me and said, "She trying to say now that I have kid with two other women. Where she get that from?"

"How long have you been married?" asked Barry.

"Fifteen years."

"And how long have you been cheating on her?"

"Fifteen years."

Everyone was in hysterics. This guy was unbelievable - his poor wife.

"Well, write down that you don't like the product and your reasons in the comment card after the presentation," said Barry.

We finished the video, but Rigoberto's loud grunts and humphs made it hard to concentrate on filling out the feedback forms.

The next product was a new type of piggybank that automatically counted coins and wrapped them in bank rolls for easy deposit.

When the "Piggy Blanketer" video started, Rigoberto started to laugh. I looked at him sternly because I wanted to hear about the product.

"What's so funny?" I whispered.

"You know when you go out to the ranch and you see a pig," he began in his heavy accent.

Now, at this point the guy went off about some really disgusting things he did with this pig in Cuba. He recounted it with such glee and vivid detail that it was like he had just done it that morning.

"I don't wanna hear it!" I shouted.

"What?" he asked. "Is normal. Everyone does it."

I sat, wide-eyed and shook my head. *No. Nobody normal does that*, I thought.

The thought of what he did to that pig... and then to cook it for his whole family! The shock of the situation distracted me from hearing anything about the product; plus, I was so disturbed I had to walk out of there. I ended up forfeiting my compensation because I didn't finish the hour. I only had to stay for another fifteen minutes, but I just couldn't.

"*Mercy bouquet* for the opportunity, but I have to go," I said to Barry.

He laughed, but I didn't know if it was at me for some reason or if he was laughing at Rigoberto. Either way, I now had to figure out how I would explain this to Mr. B. without sounding crazy.

Saturday, November 15

The Zoo

It had been more than a week and I still hadn't found Morgott. After returning from the focus group I had tacked the "missing" flyers on every telephone pole and power line post in a three-block radius from my house. I figured Morgott was too lazy to go much farther than that. During the week I ran an ad in the newspaper, I spoke with neighbors, and canvassed the entire area around my apartment building calling for him, to no avail. I was now facing the possibility that he may be gone forever. Truly this was not what I needed two weeks before Thanksgiving. I printed pictures of his fat face and put one in my car and one in my wallet so I could remember his lazy butt. He had to turn up. He just had to.

The only positive thing to happen was that during the week another guy responded to my online profile, and we had scheduled a date at the zoo.

His name was Brent, and he was not necessarily my type, being one of those meathead types, but the website seemed to think we were very compatible - and at this point I was nobody to be too picky.

Being an animal lover and missing my Morgott, I readily agreed to go. I prayed so much the night before that this would work out; I was down to less than two weeks before the Thanksgiving party.

I met him at his house, which was a modern two-bedroom single family home in a decent part of Fort Lauderdale. Outside his house, I realized the guy was a cop. His cruiser was parked out front. I sent him a text message from my car to let him know I was outside, and he opened the door and waved for me to go in. Either he wasn't ready or he wanted to show off something inside his house.

When I walked in, he called out from his bedroom, "Just hang out for a sec, I'll be ready in five minutes."

I took the opportunity to look around. He had pictures of himself all around the house, doing all kinds of outdoor activities from canoeing to mountain climbing to hiking. His friends were all meatheads too, probably all cops. In the living room he had a display shelf with pictures of himself all over the world: Paris, Rome, Chile, Brazil. He came out while I was looking at the pictures.

"Have you ever been to any of those places?" he asked.

"No, but I always wanted to visit Paris," I said.

I looked over at him and he was in a black tank top, khaki dress slacks, and dress shoes. I figured he'd changed his mind about going to the zoo.

"Okay, I'm ready. Let's roll, we have a long drive," he said.

I looked him over again. *Oh, well*, I thought, *better him than me*.

The Miami Zoo was more than forty miles away from his house and I didn't want to take my old Cutlass.

"Oh, can we please take your car? I've never been inside a cop car before," I said.

"Yeah, sure," he replied.

"*Mercy bouquet*," I said in a coquettish way.

"You know it's *merci beaucoup*, right?"

"Ha ha," I replied nervously. "Of course I do. I was just joking!"

My mother's influence seemed to permeate every aspect of my life and refused to release its grasp on my innocence. Now I had to question everything she taught me about foreign languages, including the idea that "Bone Journal" was Italian for "this meal looks great" because it was a popular magazine for the best food in Italy (she used to scream it out loud whenever we went out to eat Italian), that "Cancun" was named after an animal related to the raccoon, and that a guy named "Felix Navidad" was the Spanish version of Santa Claus. I made a mental note to look these up when I got home.

The drive down to the zoo wasn't too bad. The police cruiser was neat, with a lot of buttons that had different functions from a simple yelp to a full-on siren, to a loudspeaker.

"And what does this one do?" I asked Brent.

"Oh, that's the 'yelp' we use to open gates in communities with restricted access," he said.

"Really? You can do that?"

"How do you think we can get inside gated communities so quickly during an emergency?"

"Whoa. Too cool. How does it work?"

"It's really complicated for you to understand unless you're an officer," he said, "but it has something to do with the frequencies. You know, science stuff that you probably don't really care about."

The rest of the drive Brent talked about all the pets he'd had in his life since he was a kid, and how much he missed them all. He mentioned his love for the zoo and how he almost got hired there as a tour trolley operator when he was seventeen.

It turned out that this brutish muscle head had a sensitive, fun side that made him very loveable. A cop. Maybe he'd eventually be a spy. I imagined tagging along with him on spy missions throughout Europe – Paris! I would be his Ursula Andress, dressed in my sexy bikini and holding his gun, and he'd be the spy who loved me, in a stunning Armani tuxedo with a martini in one hand, and me in the other. Shaken... *and* stirred.

At the zoo I grabbed a map to plan our excursion while Brent paid for our admission. I was surprised at how much the zoo had changed since I was a kid. They had renamed it "Zoo Miami" from "Miami Metro Zoo", they added several acres of exhibits, and they also added a second food court.

As I looked through the guidemap, I noticed an ad for a familiar product - it was the Spectafier! Oh my God, they were selling a monkey-shaped one at the gift shop. I felt so important thinking that I was a panel member for that product, and my opinion could actually help launch it to major retailers. And to see that they sold it at the zoo -how cool was that?

"Gracie?" said a voice from behind me while I perused the guidemap.

I turned and saw a man who looked familiar. After several seconds, I realized it was Gregory Carson. He and his twin brother Vince had gone to high school with me.

"Greg! How are you? How's Vince?" I said.

"Oh, great. He's around here somewhere," he said. He looked around but Vince was probably already inside.

"Give me your phone number so we can catch up and maybe hang out," I said. Then I leaned in closer and whispered, "I'm kind of on a date, so..."

"Ok," he said, and then looked at my date. Greg made a weird face when he saw him. "Oh," he added.

"Yeah, he's a cop. Anyway," I said, giving him a kiss on the cheek, "have fun at the zoo. Tell Vince I said hi."

"Sure will. Oh and here's my card. It has my number and email."

Turned out he was now a writer. On his card he had the covers of three books, a mystery series about a dwarf detective named Tim Marrow. Interesting. A serious story about a dwarf detective. I would check it out.

I remembered hearing something on the news about Greg's brother getting into some kind of trouble, but I didn't really pay much attention to the news, so I didn't remember if I even knew what it was about to begin with.

Brent waved to me, signaling that he'd already purchased our admission tickets.

We had a great time looking at all the exhibits. My favorite was the elephants. I don't know why I like them so much, but they've always fascinated me.

We were about halfway through the zoo when we saw there was a crowd of people watching one of the exhibits. Curious as humans are, Brent and I hurried over to see what it was. Turns out it was the warthogs, and two of them were going to town mating.

"You know when you take a pig," began the voice with the Cuban accent in my head. The male warthog suddenly looked like Rigoberto, and he looked over at us in the crowd as if he was enjoying putting on the show. My stomach rumbled, then it felt like someone hit the "heavy duty" button on a washing machine in there. I quickly ran behind a tree and vomited everything I had eaten during the day. Out of me came almost an entire hotdog, which I know I chewed, darn it. It was so gross that it sent me on another wave of emesis.

Thankfully I was done and back next to Brent before he even noticed I was gone. I grabbed his arm and he turned and made eye contact with me.

"That was an interesting *sexhibit*," he said. He exposed those beautiful white teeth; his shiny black hair gleamed in the sun; and his green eyes sparkled when the sun reflected off his large, tan, sweaty biceps. This was the guy. I planned on asking him to be my date for Thanksgiving as soon as our tour of the zoo was over.

But I couldn't have guessed what fate had in store for me instead.

"Hey, wanna catch the show? It starts in twenty minutes," he said.

I should have known what would happen; I should have said "no".

"Sure," was my reply. "And maybe we can leave after that."

We casually walked to the amphitheater but when we got there we looked for seats quickly, because a crowd was gathering. We found two seats right on the front row, slightly off center.

"Ladies and gentlemen," said the announcer over the P.A. system when the show was starting, "please welcome Tammy and Joyce, our AOM Friends Trainers!"

The crowd cheered and two women dressed in khaki shorts, white tank tops, and safari hats came out on stage. One of them had a macaw on her shoulder; the other had a monkey wrapped around her chest.

"Welcome everybody," said the blonde. "My name is Joyce and this is Fanny." The macaw flapped its wings while the crowd cheered.

"And I'm Tammy," said the black girl, "and this is my friend Darren." The monkey waved at everyone, and again everyone cheered.

"*Animals on a Mission* is a group of zoo friends whose primary job is to help bring cheer into the hearts of kids with terminal illness."

Again people cheered and I leaned over to Brent and said, "Aw, that's so cool that they do that!"

He nodded.

"Well, we have many surprises in store for you today but we're going to need two volunteers," added Tammy.

I raised my hand and pointed down at Brent's head, and he shook his head 'no'. There was a rumble in the crowd and several people were trying to volunteer their loved ones, like I was.

"Ok," said Joyce, "this is a tough decision, so we're gonna have our friends Fanny and Darren select our volunteers."

The macaw took flight all the way to the back of the amphitheater; whatever I did in my past life must have been really bad, because fate led the monkey straight to me and Brent. He showed us his teeth and grabbed Brent's hand, then led him up the stage. The macaw had sat on a little girl's shoulder, who was about six years old, and stayed there until the girl's mom walked her to the stage.

"Alright," said Tammy, "what are your names?"

"I'm Suzette," said the little girl with a giggle.

"My name's Brent," said my date, waving at the crowd.

"Alright, let's hear it for our volunteers!" called out Joyce.

Again everyone cheered. I swear that show was probably only about ten minutes long but they billed it for an entire hour in anticipation of all the time spent on the crowd cheering.

So the women had Suzette do several different things with her hands and the macaw mimicked her with its wings. They did it for several minutes, and then Tammy called the crowd's attention to Brent and Darren.

"Before we retire our volunteers and bring out Rattan, our Liger, we will have Darren show Brent how to do a few tricks."

At this point Brent stepped back and didn't notice Darren behind him, so he trampled the poor animal, causing the monkey to scream in a panic. Before he knew it, Brent the cop had Darren the monkey around his waist, biting and clawing at him.

The crowd went silent as the monkey continued its assault, eventually breaking Brent's belt off and causing his khakis to fall, revealing his secret: he was wearing red lace women's lingerie and stockings under his slacks.

"No!" I screamed.

He quickly covered his essentials with both hands as Tammy rushed to retrieve a tarp so Brent could cover himself, go backstage, and get decent.

He was one of *those* weirdoes. I saw parents diving to cover their children's eyes, but it was too late; the damage was done. I followed suit and buried my face in my hands and thought, *is anyone normal anymore?*

We immediately left the zoo, and the entire walk to the car we had to bear the burden of being taunted and teased as the "weird couple" by patrons of the zoo.

On the drive home, Brent tried to make small talk, as if nothing had happened. I couldn't look at him in the face, and definitely not anywhere else, either. Horrible flashbacks of my ride with the total stranger who peed in my car monopolized my thought process, so I didn't say anything.

When we got to his house, I walked straight to my Cutlass without a word, and he didn't try to stop me.

"What is wrong with men?" I demanded of Jennifer over the phone when I got in the car.

"Oh no. What now?"

"The guy was wearing women's lingerie under his clothes at the zoo."

"I'm not even going to ask how you know that, but ok. So he's kinky. So what?"

"I didn't really like him to begin with. But it was scary. It really creeped me out. I was scared and disappointed the whole drive up."

"Gracie, listen. You're a beautiful girl, and you have such a big heart. Why are you going to settle for someone just to appease your mother? Let things happen naturally."

I then realized I wasn't really upset about Brent. I was in need of my support system. For once, I wanted things to change for the better. My job was boring, my mother was annoying, and my cat was gone.

"And Morgott. It's been over a week, and I think he might be dead."

"Oh, Grace," she said. "I'm sure he'll turn up. He's probably at one of the shelters – have you checked there?"

Had I been that stupid that I forgot to check one of the most obvious places?

"Of course I have," I lied, my tears suddenly drying up and being replaced with newfound hope.

"Well, I would canvas the neighborhood again if I were you. Anyway, I have to feed Ezra."

"Ok, Jenn. And thanks."

"For what?"

"For always being there for me."

Wednesday, November 19

The Robbery

I waited until the animal shelters opened on Monday and then called frantically in a last-ditch effort to find him, but Morgott was not in any of them. I was sure that they'd recognize him by description alone, because I knew there was no way there could be another cat like him.

It had been two weeks of searching, calling, knocking on doors in my free time, but nobody had seen Morgott.

Then on Wednesday I was leaving my house to go for a walk in the morning, when I got in the elevator with Mrs. Dunmore. She was an elderly lady who lived a few doors from me and moved around in an electric wheelchair. She didn't really need to use it, but her adult children insisted on it, and she ended up liking it. Sometimes she would crash into the wall and had to get out off of it and physically pull it back a bit to continue on her way. It was very "Three Stooges".

"Good morning, Mrs. Dunmore," I said.

"Oh, hello, Gary dear," she replied. She often thought I was her nephew Gary.

As the doors of the elevator closed, I heard a familiar sound coming from under the blanket on her lap.

"Mrs. Dunmore, what is that sound?"

"What do you mean, dear?" she asked.

"There's like a whining sound coming from your lap," I said, pointing.

She lifted her blanket and who was there? None other than Morgott, that lazy bum. Tears welled up in my eyes and I almost jumped in place until I remembered we were in an elevator.

"This is my heating blanket. Now that it's cooling off outside I use it to keep from getting sick," she explained.

"Mrs. Dunmore, that's not a heating blanket. It's my cat Morgott," I said.

"That's not a cat, dear. See?" She pinched Morgott and twisted, but he didn't react. The elevator stopped and when the doors opened, I stepped in front of her to block her exit.

"I'll help you find your heating blanket, but this is my cat. I need to put him back in my house," I said, and immediately pressed the button for the third floor.

And finally something went right for me. I skipped my walk so I could feed my cat and spend some time with him. He was lucky to be so fat that he could survive that long without food. I almost even called out from work, but this was our bank deposit day, so I had to go in. I held Morgott in my arms until I had to leave and kissed him goodbye about forty times. "Please don't do this to me again," I said.

At work I was distracted by thoughts of Morgott. I don't know why it never occurred to me that he couldn't possibly go much further than a few doors from my apartment; the cat was as fast as stone. If it ever happened again, I knew now where to focus my search.

My day would be rather easy at work because it was nearing the holidays, so supervision was more lenient, people shared catalogs and gift ideas, and workload was rather light.

I gave Mr. B the heads-up that I might be a little late from lunch because I had to stop at the bank, and of course he said he was ok with it. I took my lunch at 1:30 as usual, and hurried through the tempest with a plastic bag over my head to my car.

Now, South Florida is notorious for its unpredictable weather. It is, after all, a swamp, so it is not surprising that we get a lot of rain here. The rain started around one in the afternoon, which is not very common – it usually rains in the late afternoon, but that's

South Florida for you. In any case, I had to go to the bank to deposit my paycheck and Graduate's receivables. Well, it wasn't a bank, it was a credit union, but it was all the same, in my mind.

The bank was pretty empty. I knew that Wednesday was the slowest day, and 2:00 pm was the slowest time, so I always planned my trips accordingly, and it always worked out well.

The credit union was small, in a standalone building that used to be a Burger King restaurant. I liked that it was not a large national chain; they only had two branches. I knew all of the employees and they always treated me very well. I went straight to the desk where the deposit supplies were stacked, and I filled out my deposit slip.

On this day I was not in any type of rush, so as I filled out the slip I started some casual conversation with the security guard, Marvin.

"Hey Marvin. How did Terrence do on that spelling bee?"

"Oh just fine, Mrs. Feldman, just fine," he replied. Marvin was a black man in his early forties, and he had a ten year-old son who was very gifted. "He won second place."

"Oh, well, there's always next time," I said.

"Oh, no. We're very proud of him. Very proud. Ain't nothin' wrong with second place, now," he turned his head and lowered his chin as he said this, as if clarifying a piece of advice.

"Yes I guess you're right. It's still a great honor to win second."

Right then, a man walked into the building wearing a hoodie and sunglasses, which was odd, because the sun sure wasn't out. Marvin was still talking with his back to the front door, so he didn't notice the suspicious man, but I knew something wasn't right about him. I tried to signal to Marvin, but the poor guy was so animated in talking about his son that he didn't take notice of my signals.

Within minutes, the hooded man walked up behind Marvin and pulled out the gun he had hidden on the waist of his pants.

"What the-" was all Marvin could say before the hooded man pistol-whipped him unconscious.

I was so scared that I immediately dropped to the ground with my hands on my head.

"Oh God, oh God, oh God," I mumbled repeatedly.

"Nobody move!" called the gunman. "You," he said, waving the gun at the teller, "you touch that alarm and you die."

The teller immediately put her hands in the air, and the gunman grabbed me by the hair, pulling me to my feet. The force he used felt like he'd yanked a handful of hair off my scalp. He kept me beside him with the gun to my ribs as we approached the teller window.

"Fill up the bags. Now!" he commanded.

"Please don't hurt us," said Belinda, the teller.

She was in her eighties, and the sweetest lady I'd ever met. I felt terrible for her, thinking she might have a heart attack during the ordeal. She filled a few canvas bags full of money from her drawer and handed them to the gunman.

"There better not be an ink bomb in either of these," he said. When he reached for the bags, his hoodie got knocked back, and I got a quick look at his face before immediately lowering my gaze. That's when I realized I knew him. The golden curls were unmistakable; it had to be him. I looked back up at him.

"Memphis?" I asked. The increasing rain outside created a hurried rhythm over the silence within the bank that made the situation more tense.

He was shaken by the realization that he'd been made.

"Who?" he said.

"Oh my God, what are you doing?" I continued.

"G-Grazer? Grazer Feldman?" he said in astonishment.

I shook my head in disbelief. He had so much going for him. He could have landed a cushy job with his looks alone. What the heck was he doing robbing a bank?

"Memphis, what has happened to you?" I asked.

The sound of thunder crashed outside; it felt like it was right in front of the credit union building, because it caused all the windows to shake like the rattles on snakes.

"Ah... ah..." he said, looking in all directions, eyeing the cameras, down at Marvin, then bolting out the door before he said anything else.

I walked up to Marvin, who was trying to get up, and asked him if he was ok.

"Sure, Mrs. Feldman. I'm ok. Cops gonna be here in a few minutes, so if you could, please stick around to let them know you recognized the robber."

"I have no problem doing that, Marvin," I replied. Maybe there was justice in the world, even though it saddened me to think what Memphis had turned into.

I stayed on the floor with Marvin until the cops arrived, I gave them the information. When they keyed his name into the system, they found he had a rap sheet as long as "War and Peace". My dismay didn't end at his rap sheet; it was exacerbated by the types of charges brought against him, most still pending trial. He was accused of possession of controlled substances, armed robbery - attempted murder!

When I got home I ran a background check and found he'd had a kid with October just after I last saw him at my college graduation. I had no idea where she had gone, and I didn't really care, but I was sure glad things hadn't worked out between me and him.

Chapter 6

Thursday, November 20

The Original Copy

We were one week away from Thanksgiving, but my concern was about to have a new face. The day before Thanksgiving Graduate Plastics had to begin production for their holiday rush. I had received the approved tentative purchase order at the beginning of the month, but I didn't immediately place the order for the raw materials because we had no room to store them yet. We always placed the order two days before production was to start.

I remember putting it on my desk; it was a small, postcard-sized confirmation from the materials supplier with a price quotation and tentative purchase order. To get the material delivered on time, I had to send it, signed and dated, the day before I needed the stuff.

Since I couldn't find it on my desk, I asked around.

"Linda, have you seen a purchase order I had on my desk for raw materials?" I asked the receptionist.

"No," she said. "Ask Damaris. Sometimes she takes them to verify them."

So I asked Damaris, and she said she didn't take it. I asked Laura, and still nothing.

I looked everywhere for the purchase order. It was not on my desk. It was not in my jacket. Then I remembered I took it home because it had come through so small that I was going to take it to Clinker's to have it enlarged. I never got around to doing it, and I must have forgotten about it. I figured it was in my other jacket at home. It wasn't yet imperative to get it done that day, but the deadline was less than a week away and I needed to find it so I could get started sooner than later.

Work that day was rather dull; not that it's ever really fun, but this was a particularly slow day because none of the office staff felt like talking or anything. Everyone was anxious because the announcement for the holiday bonus was going to be made sometime that week. People wanted to get a move on holiday shopping, so they had to plan budgets, plan shopping sprees, and plan for Black Friday.

As if I really needed to clarify what happened to the invoice, I will say that yes, my mother was responsible. Surprise? No. Sucks? Totally.

The reality of it was that this particular purchase order was the most important one in the entire year. It was for raw material that we would need by the end of the month to fulfill orders of bins for retail wholesalers and distributors for the holiday shopping season. Without the purchase order, we would be unable to fulfill orders, we'd lose our biggest and most important customers, and I'd be fired for sure.

But I wasn't stressing. I assumed I'd be able to go home that day and search in my jacket and everything would be A-O-K. Of course, that's not exactly how it went down.

I arrived at home around six in the evening, ready to find the darn purchase order and take a well-deserved nap. Morgott was on the couch, of course, staring at the blank television screen.

"Hi Morgott," I called out. He didn't even look my way, he just yawned. I smiled; I was so happy to have my old friend back.

I continued, dancing merrily, toward my bedroom. The room looked a little different, but I couldn't immediately figure out why. I removed my jacket and unbuttoned my blouse; then I removed my shoes and unbuttoned my pants. I opened my nightstand drawer and pulled out my pyjamas. I was determined to have a relaxing evening.

Once dressed, I went to task in finding the purchase order. I looked through my closet, but had no luck finding the jacket I'd worn last. I looked in my laundry hamper, but oddly, it was empty. *Strange*, I thought, *I know I haven't done laundry in over two weeks*. Dispelling my stray thoughts, I went to the kitchen, then the balcony, then the living room. No jacket. *What in the heck*, I thought. *Could I have left it at work? But I would have seen it*.

Sometimes, I remember Mother saying, *to solve a problem you need to step away for a bit*. I poured myself a bowl of Lucky Charms and then I realized I had no milk. *Whatever, I'll eat them dry*, I thought, and sat down cross-legged on the couch next to Morgott. I flipped through the t.v. channels, but there was nothing good playing, so I settled for some "Friendships" reruns. Before I knew it, I was laughing, crying, and then - sleeping.

I awoke to an apparition of my mother hovering over me, talking as if I'd been awake the entire time.

"And when I tell you to do it, you need to listen. Now look at the amount of work you'll have to do," is all I caught.

As I came to, I realized that she wasn't really there, she was haunting me a different way: she was calling my cellphone. That song was driving me nuts now, but I always forgot to change the darn ringtone whenever I actually had time to do it.

"Mother?" I was still rather groggy.

"Well, who else is it going to be?" she replied.

"What is it? I was sleeping."

"I did your laundry. I put it in a basket under your bed, because I am not going to fold or put it away for you. You need to do your laundry once or twice a week so you don't have so much to do all at once. I don't know where you get it from . Your apartment is always so dirty. And make your bed, for crying out loud."

Ugh. "Mother, I'm not dirty, I'm messy. There's a difference."

"That's what dirty people always say, sweetheart."

Then it hit me.

I darted straight into an upright position. "Mother," I said slowly. "Was there a jacket with the clothes you washed?"

"Well, yes, but I checked the tags and it said it was ok to wash in the machine."

I closed my eyes and prayed that this wasn't really happening.

"Please tell me," I whispered, trying to keep calm, with my eyes still closed and dreading the answer. "Please tell me you checked the pockets before washing the jacket."

"I check all pockets."

"Oh thank God," I let out a sigh of relief. It was like when the first rays of sun peek out after a massive, turbulent tempest.

"But that jacket didn't have any pockets," she added.

"What?" I was in full-alert mode again.

"Yes, that jacket doesn't have any pockets."

"Mother. On the inside. There are two pockets on the inside of the jacket. Oh God. Oh *God*," I stood and rushed to my bedroom. While digging through the laundry hamper under the bed all I could think about was the purchase order and Mr. B. This mistake could land everyone at Graduate Plastics in the unemployment line right before the holidays. And goodbye to bonuses.

I tossed clothes to the floor and on the vanity, out of my room and into the closet; there were clothes everywhere. I realized she was right, I needed to do laundry more often, but that was not the pressing matter at the moment.

"It's near the bottom of the basket, sweetie," she said. I could hear her shrill voice emitting from the phone in my pocket as if it was on speaker. I frenzied through the rest of the pile, ignoring Morgott as he stared at me, yet knowing I looked like the possessed child from "The Exorcist".

Finally I saw the jeans jacket. I held it up; it looked brand new. She'd done a good job. Oh crap, what was I doing? The pockets!

Immediately I opened the chest flaps and dug through the pockets. Left, then right. I was frantic, praying and hoping that I didn't find it inside the jacket; searching viciously, hoping that I'd taken it out of the jacket and perhaps hidden it in the fridge or something.

But alas, my luck was such that there was no way the P.O. *wouldn't* be inside that pocket. I slowly pulled out the crumbles, the rotini-like pieces of what was once the original purchase order for Graduate Plastic's biggest orders of the year, and dropped them on the bed on top of my tears.

March, Four Years ago

The Creeper

I was so nervous. This was the first serious interview I was going to be doing in my life. In college we had a Career Center that held seminars on creating a resume and doing interviews; I attended every seminar they held. But despite all the preparation I was nervous. I tried on my very conservative navy blue pantsuit, three times the night before the interview, reviewed a list of common interview questions and my responses, and practiced my posture and expressions in front of the mirror for thirty minutes.

The morning of my interview my mother assured and reassured me that I would do just fine.

"I'm going to make you breakfast," she said. "You need to eat well before an interview so that you are sharp and strong." She also promised to drive me to my interview so that I wouldn't have to worry about finding parking or anything.

The breakfast was delicious; it was an egg omelet with onions, tomatoes, mushrooms, and delicious globules bubbly, creamy cheese. I chased it with two cups of coffee and a glass of orange juice. When I was finished, I went to the bathroom to take one final look in the mirror. Realizing I needed some touching up, I reapplied my makeup and checked to make sure I had three copies of my resume in my Portfolio and called to my mother.

"Okay, mother, I'm ready!"

"Sure honey, I'll be right there," she replied.

On the drive to the place, which was about 20 miles away, my mother just rambled on and on about what I should and shouldn't do during the interview. I was quiet the whole way.

"And you make sure to tell them that you are smart, and dedicated, and a good Jewish girl. Unless they're Muslims, then you just want to talk about how patient and submissive you are."

I simply shot glances at her. I was too nervous to argue with her.

"Oh, and if you need me to call them and give you a reference, you just let me know," she added. Then she looked me up and down and said, "And stop shaking your leg like that, they're going think you're on drugs!"

I started to speak but stopped myself. She was right; I needed to calm down or the employer would think I was weird. So I took two deep breaths and closed my eyes. When I opened them, we were at the place. It was a large industrial office, one floor, with a four-dock warehouse. The position was for Purchasing Director, and the company was called "Graduate Plastics" - a nod to the classic Dustin Hoffman film. Not that I was familiar with it, but I looked up the company's history as instructed by Lori Cochran at UF's Career Services.

"Good luck, sweetie," my mother called out when I stepped out of the car. "And after your interview - *Lo meer gayn me visem vern*!"

I didn't turn around; I didn't know if any of the employees were outside having a smoke, and I didn't want to be embarrassed on top of being nervous. Yelling stuff in Yiddish was not a good way to get me hired *or* respected at work.

It was 10:15; my appointment was for 10:30. The office smelled like a mix of gasoline and fried food. I walked inside and straight to the receptionist. She was a Cuban girl about twenty five, slightly overweight, and with a top that was very inappropriate for work, considering the size of her boobs.

"May I help you," she said, half-interested, through the open reception window.

"Hi, I'm here to meet with Darren Braddock for an interview."

"Ok, just sit down and I'll page him," she closed the window in the middle of her reply.

Looking around the small waiting room, I got an idea of the type of place this was. It was a bit old, with cracks on the walls and what looked like coffee stains on the floors. On the door that led into the office was a poster of "The Graduate" featuring a young Dustin Hoffman standing awkwardly at a doorway with his hands in his pockets, and a woman's leg in the foreground beckoning him. "This is Benjamin. He's a little worried about his future," was the tagline. *Ha,* I thought, *I'm a little worried about my future*.

I sat down and looked around at the magazines that were splayed on the table next to my seat. Most of them didn't catch my attention since they were all industry publications, but there was a catalog from Graduate. I seized the opportunity and skimmed through it, and saw they mostly manufactured stackable plastic bins. It was probably boring work, but the job paid well.

"I see you found our catalog," said a man as he opened the door from inside the office.

"Oh, yes," I said awkwardly, placing the catalog back on the table and standing up to meet the man who I assumed would be my boss.

"I'm Darren," he said, extending his hand.

"I'm Grace. Feldman. But I guess you knew that already," I replied, shaking his hand.

"Come with me," he said. He led me through the office, which housed about twenty employees, and upstairs to his private office. They all stared and whispered to each other, no doubt worried I was there to take one of their jobs.

His suite was large, and was divided into two rooms: his conference room on the right and his office on the left. Both rooms had windows from which he could watch the operation downstairs and the warehouse in the rear.

We walked into his office and he took a seat, then offered me one.

"This is quite an office, isn't it?" I asked. I felt a tickle in my stomach. *Must have been the eggs*, I thought. *Or the cheese*.

He smiled and looked around. "Yes, I suppose," he replied.

"Let's get down to business," he said as he pulled a piece of paper that I assumed was my resume, closer to his face. "I see you have no actual work experience," he said after a moment.

Before I could speak, I felt my stomach rumble. *Oh no*, I thought, *why is this happening to me now*?

"I, uh, no," I started. My stomach rumbled once again. "I am a recent graduate of UF - go Gators! - and I did very well..." I paused until the pain in my stomach subsided. "I did very well in all of my classes. I graduated *magna cum laude*."

Loud! My stomach was so loud. I wished it would stop.

"I see," he said. "So why should I hire you into our purchasing department if you have no actual experience?"

I was now visibly shifting in my seat. "I am a fast," I paused and breathed deeply. "I am a fast learner. And I'm very dedicated. I watched that movie 'The Graduate'."

"Oh good. Then you know why we named our company 'Graduate Plastics'. I like that you've taken the initiative to learn about our organization."

At this point my stomach was like the ocean in a storm, and I was rocking in my chair from right to left like Ahab in *Moby Dick*. I had to act. I squeezed my buns tightly to try and keep everything inside, and prayed that the interview be over before I reached the point of no return.

"So, Grace," he said.

"Gracie's fine," I corrected. This time I placed a hand under my butt. I don't know why I did it; I guess I thought it could help.

"Gracie," he continued. "We may require you to work extra hours during the week. How do you feel about that?"

At this point I was sweating and shifting in my seat, no doubt making him nervous. He probably thought I was having a panic attack. I had to act. I closed my eyes and remembered my mother's words: *If you ever have to let the foo foo out in public, you have to be a lady. Sit on a chair and lift one cheek up slightly. It's important that you always keep one cheek on the chair at all times. Don't worry, nobody will notice what you're doing. Once you're in the right position, hold your breath and push out slowly. It won't make a sound, I promise.*

She called this ingenious maneuver "The Creeper", and I had performed it successfully twice before. There was no doubt in my mind that I could pull it off again.

Darren looked at me quizzically. "Gracie? How do you feel about it?"

I opened my mouth, but didn't speak. I was concentrating on lifting that cheek ever so slightly. I didn't care if it smelled like eggs or cheese, or a combination of the two, as long as there was reasonable doubt as to who did it. For all he knew it could have been someone downstairs and it floated up. Determined, I finally had my cheek high enough and I pushed. I tried to push slowly but the pressure was so high that I lost control and it tore out into the office like the cannons in the "1812 Overture". Darren stared wide-eyed, and I lowered my gaze.

After several excruciating minutes of silence, he stood and spoke.

"Well, Gracie, I see you are a woman who knows what she wants. I will take your wishes into consideration. We'll give you a call once we've interviewed all the candidates and made a decision."

I stood and walked out of the office as quickly as I could. I hurried down the stairs and out the front door, ignoring the receptionist who was having a personal conversation on the phone but didn't hesitate to look me up and down with a grimace, and waving by wiggling her fingers.

Outside, my mother was sitting in the car looking at herself on the rearview mirror. She didn't notice me until I opened the car door and sat inside. She was startled.

"Oh, honey! How did it go?"

"Just shut up and drive, Mother," I replied with teeth clenched.

"Oh my goodness! What happened?"

"I don't want to talk about it, Mother."

"But you seem upset. Did he try to touch you?"

I shot a stern glance at her. "Mother! You don't even know if it was a man! Ugh," I was so frustrated I slammed my fists against my thighs.

"Then tell me what's wrong, honey," she said softly.

I tried to hold back the tears, but it was no use. They started flowing like blood from a man stabbed in the heart. I looked at her, and my lower lip quivered. "Mother, The Creeper!" I said between sobs, "The Creeper!"

She was perplexed. "What are you saying? Take a breath sweetie."

"The Creeper attacked him!"

"Oh sweetie," she said, placing her arm around me. "There will be other opportunities."

I cried all night, Mr. Braddock's face floating around in my head as I replayed the entire scenario over and over again. I don't know what I was thinking eating such a large breakfast. This was something Lori Cochran should have taught us at one of her seminars. Don't eat anything before an interview.

"Schumpkin?" asked my mother through my bedroom door. I felt guilty, because I kind of took it out on her, but in a way it was her fault. She cooked the breakfast. She introduced me to "The Creeper".

"Yes, mother?" I asked.

"Sweetheart, do you want me to get you anything?"

"No, just leave me alone."

Between The Creeper and the news the week before about my parents getting a divorce I just needed some time alone. My room was a mess, mainly because we had to start packing our boxes to move into an apartment. My mother let my father have the house because she didn't want to live in the same place where he had been with several of his mistresses.

That night I had nightmares about evil creatures being unleashed from my butt and attacking Mr. Braddock and that receptionist. The nightmares kept me tossing and turning the entire night, and I awoke in the morning after sleep-kicking the wall. My toe hurt so bad, and I realized that not getting this job wasn't such a big deal. It was my first interview, and I had my whole life ahead of me.

I decided to write a "thank you" note like they'd taught me at Career Services, and marked my calendar to do a follow-up call a week later. Who cares, I was going to push for the job, and I convinced myself I had nothing to lose.

Almost immediately after I marked my calendar, my phone rang. It was Mr. Braddock's secretary. Apparently he thought that I was trying to make a statement about the long

hours, and he liked my unwavering conviction.
I got the job.

Chapter 7

April, Four Years Ago

The Voice

My new career at Graduate Plastics was going to start the following day, so my mother told me she was going to have her friend Tess cook me a nice dinner and that she had a big surprise for me to celebrate my new adult life.

As we approached Tess's house, my mother kept insisting that I sing. I didn't know why she wanted me to sing so bad; she'd never asked me to do it before.

"Sweetie, you have the voice of a butterfly," she said.

"Mother, butterflies don't have voices. Why do you want me to sing so bad?"

"Because, Schumpkin, I love to hear your beautiful voice. It brings me such happiness."

"I don't even know what to sing, Mother."

"Just sing that song by the black girl, Whitey Houston."

"Whitney. Whitney, Mother. Have you ever considered that you might be racist?"

She chuckled. "I can't be racist, dear. I'm Jewish."

Of course. So I belted out "I Will Always Love You", and I knew it was terrible. I was still singing when we walked into the house, and surprise! The house was packed. There were friends from school, some of my mother's friends, and several people I didn't recognize.

I looked at my mother, and asked her through clenched teeth, "Why would you make me sing in front of all of these people, Mother?"

"That's the surprise sweetie. I invited Michaela Thompson and Frank Richbaum from BMI here to hear your beautiful voice."

Oh, no! "What?" I whispered in shock. "Why would you do that? I *never* said I wanted to be a singer!"

"Well, I met Mr. Richbaum a few months ago at a fundraiser your father and I went to and when I found out what he did for a living, I mentioned how your voice is like a hummingbird's."

"Yes, because all I can do is *hum*. I am not a singer, Mother!"

She ignored my comment and called out her signature line, *"Lo meer gayn me visem vern*! Let's party!"

I hung out with my friends for most of the evening. We talked about growing up, life as adults, and our plans for the future. But about an hour and a half into the party my mother stopped the music and made everybody gather around in a semi-circle.

"Now Gracie is going to perform one of her favorite songs," she said. Then she leaned closer and nudged me.

"Sing the National Anthem, Schumpkin. That's always a good one."

I looked at her in a panic and tugged at her sleeve to signal that I really wasn't prepared to do this. She pulled my hand off her blouse and smiled at me, then waved at Michaela Thompson and Frank Richbaum "from BMI".

Great. I had no idea how I was going to get out of this one, so with no other recourse, I started to sing.

"Oh, say, can you see?" I sang.

When I got to the line, "What so proudly we hailed," I drew a blank on the lyrics. So I did what any other normal girl who forgets the lyrics to the National Anthem would do: I made up words.

Yup, I sang about how "at war we don't fail" because we travel "down the river and through the woods" to "grandmother's house" and about "my Bonnie" swimming through "the ocean's red glare" and the "bombs in the air" and the disaster I knew this performance was. I wasn't even in tune or in the right key or whatever.

After the torture was over, people reluctantly clapped and Michaela Thompson and Frank Richbaum from BMI made a quick getaway.

My mother still walked around and told every attendee that I was signed to a record contract with BMI, and that my album would be released the following year. Of course, nobody believed her, but that didn't stop them from going out of their way to congratulate me and my mother, who gloated about how I was now an adult with a career and soon I would be a celebrity as well.

My grandmother, who was still alive then, congratulated me on having such a beautiful voice, and handed me what she called a "debutante present". I opened it and saw that it was a beige-colored crocheted mantle.

"Thanks, Nana. But, what is it?" I asked when I opened the box.

"It's a mantle to place over your tablecloth in your dining room. Once you get your own house, dear, you'll have something to impress the young *k'angq*s" she replied.

"Oh, wow, that's so nice. Thank you," I said. I hugged her and then headed straight to my room to hide the "red glare" that was on my face from the night of horror. I thought I'd paid for my sins by having my mother with me all the time, and then I had The Creeper appear at my interview; but that just wasn't enough for me to purge all of the things I'd done in my previous lives. Now I had industry execs listen to my angelic voice butcher the Star Spangled Banner in front of dozens of people.

I lied down and threw the mantle over my head. Tomorrow was my first day at Graduate and I couldn't allow this stupid night ruin my new job.

Friday, November 21

The Mantle

At this point I was desperate. So I did what any self-respecting desperate girl would do: I replied to the fat guy who had emailed me when I'd first joined DatesUnlimited. What the heck; I figured if he's a good guy, who cares if he's a little overweight. Besides, he could always go on a diet. I wrote a short reply that said, "Hi Jorge, I am definitely interested. Are you available to meet sometime this week?" and sent it off.

Less than three hours later, I received his reply. He must have been as desperate as I was, because he wanted to meet the next day.

Hi Gracie, I'm so glad you replied! I am definitely interested in meeting you, too and I can pick you up tomorrow around five. Cool?

Ugh, I hated having to depend on a date to take me places, especially after the Memphis and the zoo incidents, so I sent him another reply.

Jorge, I appreciate it, but if you'd prefer, I can meet you at the place. Where would you want to go?

After I sent the message, I began putting away the clothes my mother had washed for me. I'd left them on the floor in my room the whole time, and I figured this was a good time to put them away; it kept me busy, yet near the computer at all times. Within another hour, Jorge replied.

Hi Gracie. How about we meet at my place and we'll decide from there? I don't like to plan too far ahead of time because you never know if you'll be in the mood for a certain kind of food or activity, or what the weather might be on that day. Cool?

Ugh. Fine. Because my desperation knew no bounds, I sent a very quick reply that read, *Ok, send me your address. But you better not be some kind of killer or rapist.*

I really didn't care what I was going to wear or where we were going to go. I just needed to get him to agree to go to Thanksgiving with me, and then I'd break things off with him. Yes, I knew it was a little dirty of me to do that to the poor guy, but my mother left me no choice.

I was going to meet this guy and I was probably the only skinny girl to ever accept his invitation. It was like I was doing him a favor. Yeah right, all the rationalization led nowhere; I still felt guilty as sin.

I thought that maybe Jennifer could make me feel better about doing such a nasty thing to someone, so I called her.

"Hey, Jen," I said.

"Oh, hi Gracie! What's going on? How's the manhunt going?" she asked.

"Ugh. You don't wanna know."

"That bad, huh?" She asked.

"I resorted to dating the guys from my 'decline' folder."

"Oh, no!"

"Yes," I said. "I have a date with Jorge, who weighs about 472 pounds."

"Oh my God, Gracie. You can find a decent guy, man. Why are you doing this to yourself?"

I could hear her kids in the background screaming. The poor girl always had her hands full with those two.

"You don't understand. My mother will not drop it if I show up to Thanksgiving without a date."

"Why not invite one of your coworkers?"

"No way. My boss already hit on me once, and I don't want anything to do with any of the guys who work in the warehouse. They're a bunch of 'Rico Suave' Cubans in their forties who think they're all that and then some," I said, cringing at the thought.

"So when are you meeting with Shamu?"

I laughed. "We're so mean. I bet he's a really nice guy."

"Let's hope," she said. "Anyway, I gotta go. Nazir is driving me crazy. Call me after your date."

"Ok, will do, bye."

I walked into the living room and saw that the vacuum cleaner had fallen over on top of Morgott, but he didn't move. In fact, he'd fallen asleep under the vacuum. I let out a breath and picked up the vacuum and then carried him to the couch.

I had nightmares that night. I dreamt that Jorge invited me inside his house and drugged me, and I woke up in a basting pan inside his oven, surrounded by potatoes and carrots. The whole while I was in agony, I could see him salivating through the glass door of the oven. His balding head was covered with beads of perspiration that pulsated, and each had its own eyes and mouth.

When I awoke, I checked my arms and legs to make sure I was still in one piece. The nightmare haunted me the entire day, but in the afternoon I decided to make the best of the situation and I put on some cute jeans and a trendy t-shirt from the Gap. I didn't feel like going anywhere fancy, and I was sure he'd appreciate keeping things casual, too. Plus, by keeping my expectations low, I was setting myself up to not be disappointed and to be pleasantly surprised. It was a perfect plan.

The time came to go meet him and I followed the directions he'd given me in his email. He lived nearby, about ten miles from my apartment. When I pulled up to his house, I realized why he wanted to meet there. His house was beautiful. It was in a town called Lighthouse Point, which is known for its million-dollar houses on the Intracoastal. Only very wealthy people lived there.

Already well impressed, I figured this would be a great night. My imagination took me to a life of luxury aboard private jets and grand houses, and endless shopping sprees. So what if he was overweight? We could probably hire Julie Michelle, the famous celebrity trainer, to help him lose weight like she did on the hit show "Winners Are Losers". I smiled and knocked on his door; when he opened I saw he was in a suit. I was obviously underdressed.

"Hi!" I said enthusiastically.

"Nice to finally meet you, Gracie," he said. His voice was mousy, but he talked like a camel, so he was hard to understand. His lower lip pouted out and he drooled worse than Pavlov's dogs. He also breathed heavily, as if he had just run a marathon. And, like in my nightmare, he was sweating profusely.

"Come on in," he said, moving aside to let me in first, no doubt to look at my behind.

I walked around the living room, admiring the mix of classic Rembrandt and contemporary cubist Picasso paintings on his wall and looking at his living room furniture. "Nice furniture," I said. I was lying; the sofa looked dingy and old, as if it had come from a flea market.

"*Right*? It's from Rental Central," he said.

Why would a man who is apparently so well off financially rent used furniture, I wondered.

"I see," I said. I carefully sat down, and he immediately walked up to me.

"Would you like something to drink?"

"Uh, I'm ok, thanks."

He walked toward the kitchen, which I could see from where I was sitting, and he stopped and turned back toward me.

"Actually, would you like a tour?" he asked.

"Sure, I'd like that," I said, hoping a tour of his place would give me some insight into his past, present, and future.

He waved me over and I followed. He took me through the kitchen and into the dining room, which was spacious, but the table looked like an old lady's dining table. It had a beige crocheted mantel on it just like - *wait a minute!* I thought. *I couldn't be.*

"Nice," I said, discreetly walking around the table and grabbing each corner of the mantel to study it. Sure enough, one of the corners had a banana-shaped coffee stain on it. It was the mantel I had donated to the Salvation Nation! I couldn't believe it. It was such a turn-off. It wasn't so much that he shopped at a thrift store - God knows I'd bought my fair share of items at second-hand retail stores - but it was that he would place the mantel on the table where he eats *without even washing it* that bothered me so much.

"Come so I can show you where the magic happens," he said.

Ugh. "No, I'm ok," I replied. I was so repulsed by the dirty mantel, and his comment didn't help matters. I looked around and wondered what else in the house was second-hand and whether he'd washed it or not.

"Ok," he said, then walked over to the kitchen. He returned with two glasses of wine.

"Try this, sweetie," he said. "It'll give you a *cork*gasm."

He smiled at his own joke, and I politely forced myself to smile back. I took a sip, and suddenly everything got really awkward. We stood quietly in the dining room, sipping wine.

Finally he broke the silence.

"Would you like to go out on my yacht?" He asked.

He owns a yacht but rents furniture? I thought. Something wasn't adding up.

"What do you do, Jorge?" I asked.

"Me? I'm between jobs right now. Living off my disability benefits," he said.

"You don't work? So how can you afford all this?"

"I don't really own any of this. This is my friend's `grandparents' winter home, and I watch it for them until they come down in December. Then they let me stay in one of the guest rooms. The yacht is theirs, too."

Oh, no. "And they don't have furniture?"

"No. It's cheaper for them to rent some from Rental Central when they come down. That's where I got the idea to do it too. I can't wait until you meet them. They're swingers. Trust me, you'll like them; they're a lot of fun." He winked at me and stuck his tongue out several times, like a lizard.

I had to run. Quickly. I gulped down the rest of my wine and said, "Jorge, it's been really nice to meet you but I just got a text saying that my mother needs me to take her to the urgent care, because she's having a rheumatoid flare-up."

The lie was kind of ridiculous, I know, but it was all I could think of at the time. Plus, he seemed to be buying it. I stood up and tried to hand him my empty glass. He refused to take it and walked into the kitchen.

"Just text her back and tell her to get some of that Chinese ünguent from Walred's," he replied from the kitchen. "You know what it is, right? An ünguent? It's like a witchdoctor's balm, and it works like a charm on almost anything."

Really? Was this really happening to me? It was a sign.

"Uh, no. She's really not doing well. I'll email you back tomorrow, ok?" I said as I hurried out the door.

When I got in my car I noticed him at the front door, looking rather confused. It was reminiscent of Elmer's disappointed look when I left him outside the restaurant. Whatever, I didn't care. I was not at a time in my life where I could give people the benefit of the doubt. I needed a guy that my mother wouldn't tear to shreds at Thanksgiving. This guy was definitely not it. Sure, they could swap ünguent tips, but that's about it.

On my drive home, I realized this was it; this was my last chance to find a date for Thanksgiving and it was a bust. I just wanted to get home and lock myself in my room until Hanukkah.

Chapter 8

Saturday, November 22

The Advice

Now less than a week away, I called Jennifer for some words of encouragement. I really needed someone to talk to, but I wasn't about to go over to her place because I was stressed out enough without screaming children running around.

"Jen, I'm really depressed," I said.

"The last one didn't turn out so well either, huh?" she said.

"No. He lived with his friend's grandparents. He didn't work, he had no aspirations, he swings with the old couple, and he uses ünguents."

She laughed. I'd told her the story of the ünguent when I met her my freshman year at college. "What'd you guys do on your date?"

"No, no. There *was* no date. We were at 'his' house and he was giving me a tour. Then he got really creepy. He told me the wine would give me a corkgasm, and then he wanted to show me the bedroom, where 'all the magic happens'."

"Oh my God, Gracie. Why don't you try a different website like 'Hebrews For Jew' or 'The Site For Semites'?"

"Because I don't want to limit myself to just Jewish men."

"Well, there are plenty of others. Try 'Match Me.com' or 'eSymphony'. I hear those are really good."

"I don't know. How do I land a date and convince him to go to my family Thanksgiving dinner to meet my mother in less than a week? It'll scare off any decent guy."

"Don't worry about it, Gray. Just go to your mother's by yourself, then, with your head held high. In the end it's not her business anyway."

"Yeah, but you don't understand. She's like a bad outfit on prom night. You know, it's on you and you're conscious of it the entire time, but you can't get rid of it."

"Have you ever heard that Phil Collins song, 'You Can't Hurry Love'?"

"That's by the Supremes," I said.

"Whatever. He did a version of it. Just sing that song to yourself whenever she brings up your love life."

"You really think that'll work to help me ignore her?"

"Yeah, man. But look, in the end the song is right. If you force yourself to meet someone, you're gonna end up with an alcoholic or a wife beater or something."

"Yeah, you're right. But I had told her I had a boyfriend I'd been dating for several weeks. She wanted to meet him," I said.

"Oh. Why don't you tell her you got in a fight that morning?"

"No way. She'll go insane trying to figure out if he hurt me or something. Then she'll press me for his name until I spit it out. She will not shut up until I tell her *everything*."

"Why did you tell her that you had a boyfriend to begin with?" she asked.

"Because she'd been calling me for a month and I was avoiding her because I didn't wanna hear her lecture."

"Man, Gracie, you've dug yourself in pretty good. How about you skip Thanksgiving altogether?"

"Are you crazy? My mother and my aunt will be at my house faster than fruit flies at a pumpkin chucking contest. They'll think I'm sick or *worse*. My mother will probably make up a whole story in her head about me being kidnapped or something."

"Ok," she said. "I have it. Tell your mother that he is so close to his family that he had to go help his mother cook the dinner, so he couldn't go to yours. That will also give you an excuse to leave early if things get really heated."

"Hmm. That might actually work. But what if she asks for a picture of him?"

"Just tell her you didn't bring any. It should buy you another couple of weeks."

"Yeah, that may just work."

Sunday, November 23

The Worst Feeling

Although I now had a plan to stave off my mother's barrage of questions about my love life, there were other issues I had to address that week. My primary one? The darn purchase order for work.

If I didn't figure out a way to get that order in, I would be out of a job by Friday. Worse than that, I'd lose my apartment and probably have to move back in with my mother.

The main problem was that I had no clue how much raw material we'd need. I knew what a good price was and what good payment terms were, but I had no clue how much material we'd need to fulfill orders. The production manager was in charge of that, and he was Mr. B's brother. I wasn't about to reveal to *him* that I'd lost the purchase order.

I spent the entire day inside my room crying. My life as I knew it was about to be over, and I'd have to go back to live the rest of my life the way my youth was spent.

After several hours of contemplation, I had a visitor in my room. Morgott seemed to know I was feeling down, and he always knew how to brighten my day. He plopped his fat butt down on the floor in front of me and chewed on his own tail. He brought a smile to my face, and I was glad to have him back because he reminded me of how insignificant things really were in the grand scheme of things.

I picked him up and walked over to my computer. With Morgott still in my arm, I pulled up the DatesUnlimited website and clicked on "cancel my membership".

Are you sure? it asked. *Yes, absolutely sure*, I thought, then clicked the 'Yes' button. I would lose my money for the Platinum Membership, but I didn't care.

I looked over at Morgott and gave him a kiss on the forehead. He pawed at his face, as if he was wiping off the kiss. This was all the love I needed.

Chapter 9

May, Four Years Ago

The Graduation

The Commencement Ceremony for UF was going to be held at the O'Connell Center on campus. My mother and father were going to watch me walk across the stage, even though they were already going through the divorce and weren't really on speaking terms. They would be driving up in separate cars.

Herbie was also going to go, but his parents didn't care to go with him, because the cat was already out of the proverbial bag, and the love trapezoid that involved them and my parents and God knows who else made it impossible for them to want to go and risk seeing each other.

Herbie had studied Biology at Broward College in Coconut Creek, so I didn't get to see much of him while I was away in college. But we talked quite often. When I went back to live in Fort Lauderdale, we talked less and less. Now I was working at Graduate Plastics, my first real job, and I was very busy trying to find a place to live to avoid beings under my mother's scrutiny all the time.

On the drive up, Herbie and I sang along to old songs like "What's Up" from Four Non-Blondes,

"Smells Like Teen Spirit" from Nirvana, and we dorked out to "Karma Chameleon" from the Culture Club. It was like we were kids again.

"I love you Gracie," said Herbie at one point, as we pulled into a rest stop.

"I love you, too, Herbie. This is so much fun; we definitely need to take road trips more often."

He stared at me with his cherubic face, and all I could think of was how much I hoped he found a guy that would make him happy for the rest of his life.

"Alright, this is the last stop - we'll be in Gainesville in less than an hour," I said.

"Sweet. My butt is kinda numb," he said as he rubbed it.

It was already night time when we got to our hotel in Gainesville, so I met with my mother and went to bed.

The next morning I put on my cutest yellow sun dress, straightened my hair, and prettied myself up as much as possible. My mother decided to wear her glasses with the pink strand, her green blouse with a neckline ruffle, and her hair in a Marge Simpson style.

"Are you really going to need your glasses?" I asked.

"Probably not, but we are at a college, a place of higher education. I need to look more intelligent," she said.

I rolled my eyes and grabbed my purse.

We got to the O'Connell Center and met with Herbie and my father. My mother was aloof when we got there and kept looking at her watch, as if she was waiting for something to happen.

"They're late," she mumbled to herself. Then she added, "They're going to have to give me a discount."

"Who's late, mother? And why do you have to fall into *every* Jewish stereotype?"

"What do you mean? Anyway, I have a big surprise for you that I know you're going to love!" She pinched my cheek, which she knew I hated, so I rolled my eyes. *Please*, I thought, *don't let it be a surprise like the one she had for me before I started at* Graduate.

"Ooh, there they are! There they are honey, come," she said. She grabbed my hand and dragged me toward what looked like an entire production team with cameras, light umbrellas, reflectors, video cameras, and lights. One guy even carried a fan.

"Mother, you *didn't*," I said.

"Of course I did! Anything for my special little Schumpkin."

I turned to Herbie for help, but he put his hands out and shrugged his shoulders, as if saying, "I got nothin'."

"Lo meer gayn me visem vern!" said my mother. "Let's party!"

The camera crew took up the entire front row during the ceremony. I found out later that she had paid them $20,000 for the production, which included photo books and a DVD. Sure, the end result was nice, but it wasn't like this was my wedding. I was graduating from college for God's sake.

My father wasn't happy about the frivolous way my mother spent his money, but he was in no position to say anything after cheating on her with two women, and maybe more.

After the ceremony, the camera crew followed me all throughout campus. They even filmed us while we ate lunch. Some of the kids thought I was a celebrity; those were probably all freshmen. Most of the other kids just laughed when they passed us. Luckily I would never have to see most of those people again.

October and Memphis passed us, too, and made sure to laugh as loud as possible, mooing and heeing and hawing to embarrass me. I ignored them, because they did belong together and I figured I'd never see them again either unless they became models or movie stars.

Although that day was embarrassing, I cherished the memory of it because it was the last I ever heard of my father and the last time I saw Herbie.

Tuesday, November 25

The Junction

My mother's words of discouragement floated around in my head. She hadn't said them yet, but I knew they were coming. Thanksgiving was panning out to be hell on Earth. I was so depressed I didn't feel like talking to anyone.

I felt like a crazy person; on one hand, I was determined to tell my mother she had no business delving into my love life. On the other, I wanted to have that life. Not for her, but for myself.

I tried to do what Jen recommended with the Supremes song, but the words kept changing in my head.

You must hurry love, you know you can't wait.

Ugh. I tried to focus on my work, but the purchase order was due to be signed and sent off that day. I sucked up my pride and walked up to the receptionist, Linda.

"I am desperate. We could all end up without work if I don't find this purchase order," I said.

"What do you mean?" she said.

"I can't find the purchase order for Malton. I had it on my desk and now it's gone." I wasn't about to admit, especially to her, that I had taken it home.

"So you still can't find it? And you didn't think to make a copy?" she said.

"You know we don't have a copier. What office doesn't have a copier?" I was rationalizing, but I really wouldn't have been in this predicament if our office had their crap together.

"We've done ok without one for many years," she said. She shrugged her shoulders, then got up and walked away.

Sometimes Linda was friendly, sometimes she was worse than Maleficent. I knew she was planning on opening a business with her father, but did she really not care if she and everyone else in the office was left without a job just before the holidays?

"So what did Ron say at Malton when you called to ask them to resend the copy?" she asked.

Of course, I hadn't thought to call them, and now it was too late. Why did Linda have to make sense?

My day at work dragged like the butt of a laughing hyena. I excused myself to the bathroom at least a dozen times to cry.

At 3:45 Linda came over to my desk just as I was about to head to the bathroom again.

"Still no P.O.?" she asked.

"No, and I don't know what to do. Is there somewhere I can get last year's P.O. so I can just duplicate that order? I now it won't be the same amount of material, but better that than no material at all. Or should I just tell everybody to start looking for work this weekend?"

"Oh, don't be so dramatic, Gracie. Nobody's getting fired."

"Believe me," I said, now crying. "We will all be out of work if I don't do something."

Linda rolled her eyes, and Damaris came over to see what was going on.

"Honey, what's wrong? Did Mr. Braddock hit on you?"

"What? No! Where did that come from?" I asked.

"It just seemed like you were upset, like a man did you wrong," she said.

"No. I'm just stressing out about seeing my mother on Thursday."

"Ok, well, I'll leave you two alone so you can talk." She didn't believe me, and went straight upstairs to reassess her position as his main squeeze.

If she only knew he was seeing everyone else in the office, including Linda, she'd have a heart attack. I was definitely not the biggest threat to her little affair.

"She's so freaking annoying," said Linda as Damaris walked away.

"What am I gonna do?" I asked, going back to the topic at hand.

"Ok, look. Come to my desk, I have something for you."

I was confused. What did she have up her sleeve this time? Curious, I followed her to her desk at the front of the office. She opened her drawer and retrieved an opened envelope. It had the Malton logo on the outside.

"You owe me big time," she said, handing the envelope to me.

I pulled the document out of the envelope and saw that it was a copy of the Malton purchase order. I was confused.

"They always send two copies in the mail; one for accounting and one for purchasing. Accounting always asks me to file it for them.

How did you not know this after working here for four years?"

"I... I don't know what to say."

"A thank you would be nice. I just saved your ass."

"You let me stress for a week, knowing I was going crazy looking for this purchase order and you had a copy all along?"

"You know what? Whatever. Maybe I should just take it back," she said, leaning closer to me with hand extended.

"No, please. Thanks for giving this to me. Now I can breathe easily."

She lifted her chin up in the air and sat down. I hurried to my desk to grab my purse so I could run to Clinker's and make a copy and then personally deliver the signed purchase order to Malton.

"Please tell Mr. B. I'm going to Malton to make sure we get delivery tomorrow," I said to Linda.

"Uh huh."

I hurried out to Clinker's - at least I would have a job after this weekend (thanks in small part to Linda), which was a relief.

When I got there, I was almost out of breath from the stress and from running as if they were going to close, even though they were open 24 hours. Thing is, Malton wasn't.

I told the girl at the counter to blow up the image twenty times so that there were no mistakes in interpretation. While I waited, I saw a cute guy waiting to pick up a poster print.

He had deep, sapphire-blue eyes and sharp, manly facial features. He was dressed in a light blue polo shirt and black slacks. He caught me staring.

"Hey!" he said.

Embarrassed, I quickly averted my eyes.

"Gracie?" he asked.

I looked up at him, somewhat confused. I was sure I didn't know him.

"Gracie, it's me, *Herbie*." The name seemed to come out of his mouth in slow motion.

The clouds parted and light came down upon me. Of course! Now I recognized the voice, although it was a little deeper than I remembered it.

"Oh my God!" I said. "You look so good!"

"I lost 210 pounds," he said.

"Wow," I said. "How'd you do it?" I was in such shock, and he looked so darn edibly good. Gay guys always do.

"Diet and exercise. You know, the old-fashioned way. What have you been up to? Are you working?" he asked, analyzing at my outfit.

"I'm at a place called Graduate Plastics. How 'bout you? Do you have a partner?"

"Partner?" he asked. Then he got a look of realization. "I didn't study law. Biology, remember?"

"Oh no, that's not what I meant. I don't know what you guys call each other now, or is it legal to get married?"

"Gracie, what in the world are you talking about?"

"I guess what I wanna ask is if you have a boyfriend."

"What?" he seemed genuinely shocked. "Not you, too. I'm not gay, Grace."

Oh. I felt so stupid.

"I had a crush on you since middle school," he said.

Double oh. "Right. I meant, are you married? Kids?"

He smiled. How could I be so Good-doggied stupid?

"Nope, still single. How 'bout you, Grace - you married?"

"Unfortunately, I'm still single too," I said.

"How's your mom?" he asked.

"Ugh, don't even ask. She invited me to Thanksgiving and drilled me about who I was dating. She even asked me if I was secretly a lesbian!"

Oh geez. Here I brought up the gay thing again. He laughed. I couldn't resist, so I laughed, too.

"I had no idea you had a crush-"

"Here you go, Mrs. Feldman," said the girl at the counter, handing me the copy I asked for.

"Oh, thank you," I said, handing the girl five dollars. "Keep the change."

I looked at the clock on the wall behind the counter and saw that I only had 20 minutes to get the purchase order delivered to Malton.

"Oh my gosh, Herbie. We need to exchange phone numbers and catch up on things, but I have to go," I said.

"Yeah, sure. Here's my card," he said. *Herbie Anderson, Marine Biologist*, it read.

Wow. So he'd done it. He fulfilled his dream, and here I was a Purchasing Director at Graduate Plastics. I decided that after Thanksgiving, I'd look for a job as a Purchasing Director at a premium clothing retailer. There was no reason to continue living the life my mother wanted me to live.

I rushed to the door and looked back at him. "I promise I'll call you tonight - answer the phone!"

And off I went.

I rushed to Malton with the purchase order, and got there exactly at five o' clock. It was a relief knowing that everything would be ok. But, as I left the place with the receipts and contract, the wind picked up. I stood in the parking lot and looked back at the sign on the face of the building. *Malton: Your Future Awaits,* it read.

Then a gust of wind kicked up behind me, and grabbed my hand, and I knew what to do; I let go of all the paperwork they had given me. The pages blew away with my cares, with the wind. I walked away, and knew I would never return.

The One?

I called Herbie that night and it was like we had never been apart. Only this time I felt more of a connection than before. We had such similar upbringings, and we'd both emerged pretty well-adjusted adults, all things considered.

"My God, Herbie you have no idea what I've been through in the last month."

"Really? What kind of stuff?"

"Well, besides the fiasco at work that I was trying to fix when I ran into you, I've had the worst dating record of all time."

"Ha ha. I love hearing dating nightmare stories. So who have you met? Backyard Rambo? A black skinhead?"

"Oh now that would be hilarious. But yeah, kind of. No, I met an unemployed guy who lived with his friend's grandparents."

"Oh, Norman Bates's cousin?"

"Almost. He told me he wanted me to see the bedroom where all the magic happens, after having a 'corkgasm' with him."

"Oh my God. Was the bedroom his or his friend's grandparents'?"

"I didn't wait around to find out. But he practically invited me to swing with them."

"With the old people?"

"Yes! Isn't that *sick*? Oh, and then there was the mustache."

"Who?"

"A guy who looked good on his profile and when I met up with him, he had a Tom Selleck-like mustache. It was like a scrubbing brush right smack in the middle of his face."

"Oh, why wouldn't he update his picture?"

"No, the problem is that I'd never kissed a guy with a mustache. So I *licked* it."

He fell into hysterics. "Gracie! *What* is wrong with you?"

"I don't know, man. I'm just glad this month is almost over so I could move on with my life."

"Well, I've dated my fair share of whackos too."

"Please tell me."

"Ok, there was the girl who liked to cut herself."

"Oh that's so sad," I said. "There are so many girls that do that nowadays."

"Yeah, but I wonder how many of those rub peanut butter on the open wounds?"

"Whoa."

"Wait, it gets worse. There was a girl that liked eating hair. She wanted to shave my head and sprinkle the hair on her pizza."

"Oh my God. That is weird, ha ha ha. I wanna hear more."

"One liked to smell my shoes."

"Oh my God! So it's not just me!"

"Yeah. We were in the middle of dinner at a fancy restaurant, and she reached under the table, removed my shoe, and sniffed it in front of everybody. I didn't know where to hide my face. But even worse, she finished with that one, handed it back, and then asked me for the other one."

"Whoa, buddy. You're almost as bad as me."

"So what's the deal with Thanksgiving?" he asked.

"My mother started asking questions about who I was dating, so I told her I had a boyfriend. She invited me to Thanksgiving and now she wants to meet him."

"Why would you do that?"

"I don't know. I didn't wanna hear her lecture about being single past thirty. You know, the whole lesbian thing."

"But she still lectured you."

"Yeah," I said.

"Well, I don't have plans for Thanksgiving. What if I go with you as your date?"

Oh my God. Could it be?

"Yes!" I didn't mean to scream, but I couldn't hold it in. "Sorry sorry. Yes, oh my God, yes. You have no idea how great that would be. Please go with me."

"So it's a date," he said.

"Yeah, I guess it is."

I finally had a date for Thanksgiving - one that I wasn't worried would bolt out the door upon meeting my mother. We continued to laugh, telling each other stories of what we'd been through these past four years; we talked about the present; we talked about the future; we talked until two in the morning.

Chapter 10

Thursday, November 27

The Party

We stood at the door and I took a deep breath. I held Herbie's hand tightly and looked him in the eyes. He smiled a gentle smile, and I smiled back. I knew everything would be okay; Herbie had been there with me in the past no matter what. But I was worried because I very well knew my mother's incredible power to destroy everything I ever wanted or loved.

Worse yet, my Aunt Janice would be there as a henchman. How could I even stand a chance? I had to push through, and Herbie was the man to do it with me. With new determination, I rang the doorbell.

Memories of all of the events of the past month ran through my head, but today seemed different. I was ready to quit Graduate Plastics after four years, and was determined to find a job with Macy's or Bloomingdale's or Calvin Klein. Or Michael Kors!

I could hear voices inside the apartment. There were a few other people besides my mother and Aunt Janice. But my mother's voice was unmistakable when I heard her say, "Ooh, that's Gracie with her new boyfriend!"

Whatever the night would bring, I was ready to face it. Or so I thought.

When the door opened, my eyes went wide, and I lost my breath - I almost fainted. My mother and my Aunt Janice were dressed in full Indian regalia, complete with headdress and war paint. They simultaneously placed their hands over their mouths and began to 'wah'. My mother then began to speak, but continued placing and removing her hand from her mouth while she spoke.

"Ha-a-a-a-a-ppy-y-y-y-y Tha-a-a-ankksgi-i-i-i-iviiii-i-i-ing!" she chanted.

I quickly pushed Herbie inside and darted in behind him so I could quickly close the door.

"Mother!" I whispered loudly. "Do you not see how *racist* this is?"

She seemed legitimately confused. "What? We're celebrating the day of giving thanks! Like the Indians and the Pilgrims did in the beginning of time."

Oh Christ, I should have believed in you so you could save me from this purgatory. I looked at Herbie and he had a smile like the Joker in Batman.

"You didn't tell me your mother was a member of the Village People," he whispered.

I teasingly poked him on his ribs and felt how meaty his midsection was. He'd gone from six packs of doughnuts to six-pack abs.

"Oh my goodness," said my mother, "is that you, Herbie?"

"Hi Mrs. Feldman," he said, and gave her a kiss on the cheek.

"Have you met my Aunt Janice?" I asked him.

"Nice to meet you, I'm Herbie" he said, extending his hand.

"Ay, yeh. Herpes. I know you so much," she said, ignoring his hand and going in for a hug and a kiss. Herbie was almost two feet taller than my aunt, but she didn't care. Her headdress rubbed all over his face as she pulled his face down for the kiss. "Tu sabes que Mallory she love todas las boyfriend de Gracie."

Herbie smiled and nodded, then looked to me for a translation. I shrugged my shoulders.

"Come, let's get something to drink," I said pulling Herbie away from my aunt.

We said 'hi' to the other guests and went into the kitchen. I stood in front of Herbie, grabbed his hands, and looked up at him. I tried to imagine my future life with him the way I'd done with all my other disastrous dates, but I couldn't. All I could think about was this moment.

"Wow, the food smells delicious," he said.

"You're standing in front of the girl you've had a crush on your entire life, holding her hands, and you're thinking about *food*?"

"Ha ha, you're right. I'm just feeling awkward. I've never, well, you know. I've never had a girlfriend before."

"Well, that makes two of us," I said.

"I sure hope not," he teased.

I poked him in the stomach. "Stop it, you jerk!"

My mother then walked into the kitchen, and my Aunt Janice was behind her, hopping from one leg to the other, doing the stereotypical Indian war dance.

"Schumpkin," said my mother, "offer Herbie something to drink."

Before I could tell her that I had already done so, she began listing stuff.

"We have sodas, juice, water, wine, punch, Manischevitz, beer, and milk. Whateva his smitten heart desires."

"Mother, who would drink milk with their Thanksgiving dinner?" I said.

"I don't know, honey. Kids nowadays do all sorts of weird things because of what science has discovered in the new millennium."

"Oh, thank you Mrs. Feldman, but I'm allergic to milk," said Herbie.

"What? To milk? You see, sweetie? It's the popular thing nowadays to do everything differently."

"Yes, mother. I see what you mean." I rolled my eyes but her idiotic comments didn't seem to bother me as much as they used to anymore.

"So you live in Tampa," said Herbie to my aunt.

"I'm unemployment, because my husband is the army."

"Oh," said Herbie. "Great!"

I served our drinks and pulled him to the living room. Perhaps the other guests could serve as a buffer and maintain some sanity in the house.

There were a total of five other people present, mostly old friends of my mother whom I'd met throughout my life. One man, in his late 80's, was my mother's next door neighbor John, who had no family in Florida so my mother always invited him to her parties.

"Lo meer gayn me visem vern," said my mother as she danced into the living room. "Let's party!"

"Mrs. Feldman," said Herbie. "You know that means 'let's go get high', right?"

"What? No, it means let's party! My father used to say it all the time, and he was from Israel, you know," she said.

I tapped Herbie with my elbow, and when he looked at me I shook my head. There was no need to correct her. She was set in her ways, and nothing would change that.

Music started to play on the radio, and Herbie and I danced to songs like "Walk Like an Egyptian", "Blame It On the Rain", and "Can't Touch This". We were having such a great time that a couple of the other ladies joined in the fray.

My Aunt Janice then walked into the living room with little baggies for each of the guests and handed them out.

"I got this en el Bed Bath and Body Works. Is good. Looki," she said, pulling out a portable bottle of hand sanitizer from her bra, pouring a generous amount on her hands, rubbing her hands together, and then patting her face. It looked like a man putting on aftershave.

"Oh thank you," said Herbie.

"Thanks Aunt Janice," I said, holding back the laughter.

The other guests thanked her also.

"Wow, this smells really nice," they all said, following suit and rubbing the stuff on themselves exactly the way my aunt had done.

"Isse Pum-king flavoring," she said proudly.

Aunt Janice then removed her headdress and held it between her legs, then poured herself a little more of the hand sanitizer. She then combed it through her short, curly brown hair with her fingers.

The guests looked at each other, and Dora, one of my mother's oldest friends, said, "I don't think I want to put this on my hair."

Tess, another one of my mother's friends, said, "I don't know if she'll be offended or if it's rude not to do it." So she did it.

John did it, too, but I'm not sure he knew what was going on. He was almost completely deaf. The other guest, Issa, had her hand on John's lap, and she mimicked everything he did. It was kind of cute seeing her try to seduce him.

Lori, another one of the guests, tried to draw attention from the fact that she wasn't putting it on her hair by asking my aunt, "So how are the kids and the grandkids?"

"Ay, good. They is good. Danto growing so fast que I cannot see el todo," replied my aunt as she placed her headdress back on.

Nobody knew who 'Danto' was, but we figured it was either Daniel or Damien. They were both her grandchildren, but she always changed everyone's names, so who knew.

"Do you have any kids?" Lori asked Herbie.

"Yeah I have a dog named Magnus," he replied. "Do you have kids or pets?"

"Oh, no. I don't need that hassle," she said.

"Don't say that about his doggy, Lauris. You don't meeti him, and you calling him an hassole?"

"No, Aunt Janice, I don't think that's what she meant," I started to say.

Just then, my mother walked back into the living room.

"Ok, everybody, dinner is ready," she said. "You can grab plates in the kitchen and follow on to the dining room to serve yourselves, buffet style."

Herbie and I got up, but waited for everyone else to serve themselves first before we attacked the buffet. It all smelled so good, I didn't know how I was going to fit everything on one plate. The good thing about Herbie was that I could be myself around him without worrying if he thought I was being a pig by eating two or three plates of food.

Herbie was very modest with his portions, though. Maybe he was worried that I would think he was going back to his old self, but I really didn't care even if he did. He was a great catch in every respect.

We sat down and my mother led the prayer.

"Oh God, thank you for allowing us to gather here amongst friends to celebrate the Thanksgiving. We love this food, we love each other, and we love you. *Mazel tov* and *lo meer gayn me visem vern!*"

Dora and Tess did the sign of the cross, while John and Issa held their wine glasses up in the air. Lori, Herbie, and I nodded at each other, and my mother and Aunt Janice held each other's hands and smiled.

"Ok, let's begin!" said my mother.

The food was delicious. I had a little bit of turkey with gravy and cranberry sauce, some sweet potato with marshmallows, mashed potatoes, and my favorite, green bean casserole.

For dessert there was Dutch apple pie, pecan pie, and, as my aunt would say, "pum-king" pie. I was really looking forward to the desserts, but when I stood up to serve myself a second helping of food, I noticed Herbie was sweating and his face was flushed.

"Oh my God, are you okay?" I asked.

"I'm fine, I'm just feeling a little warm," he said.

"I'll get you some water."

I went to the kitchen and put ice in a cup, then I heard a loud crash and a woman shrieking. I ran out to the dining room and saw Herbie on the floor, grabbing at his throat, kicking his legs. Half of the tablecloth came down with him, covering him in food and drink.

The women were screaming frantically, "Oh, my God, he's dead!" and, "Oh, I've seen this before - it's a drug overdose!"

Issa was making out with John and they were ignoring the whole thing, as if they were in their own private little world.

My aunt Janice had removed her headdress and was attempting CPR, but she was using her tongue; I thought she was making out with Herbie. It wasn't because she wanted him or anything, I thought that she truly believed that's how it was done.

Then I saw he had broken out in hives, so I called out to my mother, "Call an ambulance! He's having an allergic reaction!"

I looked at my aunt, who was rubbing Herbie's head. She'd made most of the food, so I asked, "Was there milk in any of that?"

She nodded and smiled, and said, "Yeh. Is good, ah?"

My mother ran out of the room and came back with the phone and her famous Epi Pen. She handed the phone to my aunt.

"I already dialed them, just tell them to come over quickly," said my mother, while preparing to stab Herbie in the heart with the Epi Pen.

My aunt grabbed the phone and said, "Yeh, we needi you doctor for Herpes."

What was my mother thinking giving the phone to my aunt? Without hesitation, I grabbed the phone out of my Aunt Janice's hands and told the operator exactly what was happening and to send an ambulance right away.

In the meantime, my mother had ripped the buttons off of Herbie's shirt when she opened it, and was preparing to stab him. *Careful,* I thought, *that needle might break on those strong, manly pecs*.

Then I realized what I was doing. How could I think of that when he was about to die!

"Please be careful, mother," I said, the memories of Bones convulsing and dying in my arms flashing clear in my mind.

She plunged the needle into his chest; I heard a cracking sound, and then his body jerked for several seconds, then stopped.

After a dramatic pause, he sat up and took a deep breath, as if he'd been under water for several minutes. It was like magic.

"No, lie down sweetie," said my mother, pushing him back into a lying position.

When she looked up and saw the table was almost completely cleared out, Issa asked from across the room, "Is it time for dessert?"

I fell to my knees and my mother sat back on the floor, still holding Herbie's chest. My Aunt Janice was smiling, and said, "Suerte que we habi the medicina for the Herpes."

We all looked at each other and all of the tension and worry from the past month was carried off with the laughter that ensued.

Issa looked in the fridge and said, "No more milk!"

Little did she know that her words would ring true in my house forever after that.

Later, as the ambulance carried Herbie away in the stretcher, I looked over at my mother in her Indian getup and smiled. She nodded as she gave the details of the evening to the police and the paramedics, and the whole while the feathers of her headdress bounced, as if nodding in agreement.

It was then that I finally realized that, despite all her weirdness, all her crazy ideas, all her impudence, and all her embarrassing acts, my mother was an O.K. gal.

** Continue reading about Gracie's misadventures on the new episodic series:
Morgott, Mallory, and Madness: or, Is this *REALLY* My Life?!?

at: www.GracieFeldman.com

We hope you enjoyed **Milk, Turkey, and Neurosis: or, How Mother (Almost) Ruined My Life**

If you have a moment, please go to **Amazon.com** and **Goodreads.com** to post your opinion and rate it.

For more of Gracie's misadventures, follow her on the new episodic series: **Morgott, Mallory, and Madness: or, Is this *REALLY* My Life?!?**

www.GracieFeldman.com

If you have feedback for the author, please see her contact information on the last page of the book

Grace Ann Feldman is an avid lover of cats, the kooky, and her mother, Mallory. She studied Creative Writing and English at Southern New Hampshire University and has written numerous articles in publications throughout the world. She lives in Fort Lauderdale, Florida with her cat Morgott and her boyfriend Herbie. This is her first novel.

@TheGraceFeldman
@: GracieFeldman@gmail.com

www.GracieFeldman.com

Printed in Great Britain
by Amazon.co.uk, Ltd.,
Marston Gate.